SHE

and the adventure of
The Martian War

Doug Murray

SHERLOCK HOLMES
and the adventure of
The Martian War

DOUBLE DRAGON

A DOUBLE DRAGON PAPERBACK

ISBN 978-1-78695-449-7

Double Dragon
is an imprint of
Fiction4All

Published 2020
Fiction4All
www.fiction4all.com

PUBLISHER'S FOREWORD

For the purists among you who believe that no author other than the much-famed Sir Arthur Conan Doyle has the right to write about the adventures of the great Sherlock Holmes, this foreword is for you.

In the UK in the year 2000 a court ruling made the character of Holmes and the writings of the author, public domain, meaning anyone could write books such as the one you are about to read.

A ruling in the US in 2013 has had much the same effect in that country. For those interested in such matters we would refer you to the following articles:-

https://www.smithsonianmag.com/smart-news/sherlock-holmes-now-officially-copyright-and-open-business-180951794/

https://artsbeat.blogs.nytimes.com/2014/06/17/conan-doyle-estate-loses-sherlock-holmes-copyright-appeal/

So with great admiration for those who have gone before, for those who will doubtless come after, and without more ado…

AUTHOR'S NOTE

To all of you who have the power to read and the strength of mind to care.

It has been drawn to my attention that, with her Majesty's government decreeing that this document be treated as 'Most Secret' for some time to come, many of those who read it will have already been exposed to another, quite different, account of the Martian Invasion in London—the account rendered by Mr. Wells in his best-selling novel, 'The War of the Worlds'.

Mr. Well's book, while entertaining, is, for the most part, a fiction ordered by the same government that is withholding this account. They believe—and I am forced to concur—that the world is not at this time ready for the true and quite horrid details of what happened during the brief period when Martians roamed the streets of London and preyed upon its citizens. Hundreds of thousands of people lost their lives and many who survived, did so by simply hiding until the Invasion was crushed.

It is my hope that those who survived, and their descendants, will be ready for the true facts of this Invasion after one hundred years have passed. Time is a great healer, and, one can hope, a hundred years can heal a great deal.

I can only hope that those of you reading this are capable of understanding the reason for the secrecy—and are, at the same time, strong enough to comprehend the true horrors of that time.

I also hope that there has been no further occurrence of the events noted within.

John H. Watson, M.D.

CHAPTER ONE

Sherlock Holmes sighed as he opened the door to the common room and found his friend and room-mate, Dr. Watson, at breakfast.

"You're up early, Watson. I had thought your late night might have caused you to sleep in today."

"Woke up early today, Holmes." Watson dabbed his toast into the yolk of an egg. "Felt Too hungry to go back to sleep." He looked at Holmes Gladstone bag. "Where are we off to, Holmes?"

He pushed away from the table allowing Holmes to see that a bit of egg yolk had landed on his friend's tie.

"I can be ready in just a few minutes…"

""I know you are quite busy in your surgery, my friend," Holmes noted holding up a hand. "And as my business is in no way pressing, I thought I'd go on this expedition alone." The tall man pulled a magazine from his jacket pocket and tossed it onto the table, nearly upsetting Watson's coffee cup. "Have you seen the latest issue of NATURE?"

"Why, no." Watson settled back into his chair and peered at the thick magazine before him. "It's not on my regular subscription list…"

"Look here," Holmes opened to a dogeared page. "The astronomers at the Lick Observatory say they have observed a great burst of light on the planet Mars!"

"I thought you knew nothing of such matters," Watson replied, puzzled by his friend's interest.

“I have not needed this sort of information in the past, but recently, I have been corresponding with Perrotin of Nice on another matter,” he shrugged. “In the course of that correspondence, the good Doctor was kind enough to inform me of the sighting of this ‘light’ and its possible significance.”

“Significance?”

“Not yet apparent,” Holmes waved the thought away with a too-innocent smile.

Watson didn’t notice, being intent on his breakfast he let the detective continue.

“However, on his advice, I have decided to do a bit of research. I shall journey to… “Holmes half-lifted the magazine. “Ottershaw, where I will have a chat with Olgilvy, the chief astronomer there.” The tall man straightened and turned toward the door. “At the very least it will give me the opportunity to study the so-called ‘red planet’ through the observatory’s great telescope.” He shrugged. “I know it means nothing, but as there is no interesting crime in London at the moment, I am bored. He opened the door. “I will tell you everything upon my return.”

***

A few hours later, Holmes began to wonder if it was wise to give Watson his promise to report all. The window of his first-class compartment showed the English countryside flashing by at quite a rapid rate—he had calculated that they were making at least thirty miles to the hour—quite fast for such a backwater route.

Holmes wondered if he should mention the shocking speed when he did speak to Watson again.

It's good that we are moving so fast. Homes thought., *the scenery is quite boring...*

He returned to his copy of NATURE and began, once again, to study the report on the Martian disturbances.

In a few hours, he thought. I shall be with Professor Olgilvy and, if he cooperates, I will be able to find out if any of my suspicions are correct.

Holmes put the magazine down and gazed at the sun-lit English countryside rushing by.

He sighed.

But I fear that will not be the case.

***

Professor Olgilvy met Holmes at the station and took him back to his fine house. Holmes' eyes were drawn to the oddly-shaped building that held the Professor's telescope but Olgilvy insisted that they have dinner first.

The food was quite good, perfectly cooked and served by the Professor's housekeeper. Holmes congratulated her and expressed his appreciation for the meal.

Then Olgilvy yielded to his guest's curiosity and led him out to the home of his powerful telescope, training it on the mysterious Red Planet that Holmes was so interested in.

Mars red face was in the center of the telescope's focus, quite clear, as Holmes leaned into the eyepiece.

"I see the 'canals' I've heard so much about," he reported.

"They are quite interesting," Olgilvy replied. "But I do not think they are 'canals' in the sense you mean." The professor shrugged as Holmes glanced his way. "That, Mr. Holmes, is a dead world. No water, little air—not habitable in the way the word 'canals' suggests."

"I see," Holmes replied, eyes still on the telescope. "And the mysterious explosions that have been so widely reported?"

"I have no explanation for them, Mr. Holmes." He smiled. "And they do not appear every day." He took a quick look into the lens. "It might be best if we travelled a few miles and visited Professor Pierson who has an even more powerful telescope then this and has, himself, reported on several of the 'explosions' in question." He nodded toward the house. "That article in NATURE was, in fact, his work"

"Will he welcome such a visit? I am, after all, a stranger."

"You are no stranger to any Englishman, Mr. Holmes. Of that I am quite certain." The good Professor smiled. "I will send a footman off with a message straightaway and we will proceed to his home early tomorrow morning," he looked at Holmes. "At least, if such a plan is agreeable to you?"

"More than agreeable." The detective nodded. "I am most indebted to you, Professor."

"Tell me that again," the Professor smiled wryly. "*After* you taste my cook's biscuits!"

The two laughed as they made the short walk back to the Professor's home.

***

A few minutes after midnight, Holmes was jolted awake by a roaring sound--not unlike the sound made by a speeding train. His first thought was that such a train had de-railed on the nearby railway, but he quickly realized how impossible that would be and, fully awake, fought his way clear of the unfamiliar covers and stumbled to the single window of the Professor's guest room.

He saw nothing at all and quickly realized that whatever had caused the noise was gone—and he had missed the opportunity to see what it was.

But perhaps not! He thought as he rushed downstairs, reaching the kitchen just as Professor Olgilvy burst in. "Did you see it, Professor?" he cried.

"No, Mr. Holmes." The Professor shook his head sadly. "It was gone before I could reach a window."

"What do you think it was?"

"I believe it must have been a meteorite—a rather large one." He shrugged. "With luck Professor Pierson will have seen it—he is often active late into the night."

"Have you heard back from him?"

"Indeed, we are welcome at his home at any time." The Professor glanced at the clock on the kitchen wall. "Let us return to our beds—I would prefer to travel *after* the sun has risen."

Holmes nodded, "that would be my preference as well," he replied and followed the older man up the stairs, returning to his bed and firing up his pipe to think about what he had learned.

He got no more sleep that night.

***

The trip to Professor Pierson's laboratory was uneventful although longer than expected due to the unusually large amount of traffic moving along what was, to Holmes eye, a simple country road. Early morning news told us that the object we had heard had, indeed, been a meteorite and that it came to earth somewhere not far from our destination.

"I'm sure Pierson is already investigating," Olgilvy told Holmes. "We may have to journey directly to the crater."

"Whatever you say, sir." The great Detective replied, watching the crowd around them. "Whatever you think is right and proper."

Holmes nodded to his side as a lightly-laden wagon sped past. "What do you make of those vehicles? They seem to be moving away from the excitement."

"People fear what they do not understand, Mr. Holmes." He made a dismissive gesture. "Surely you are aware of that."

Holmes nodded and shrugged as they continued on. Less than an hour later the two men reached the home of Professor Pierson who, they soon learned, had been waiting for them.

"Gentlemen," he called as we pulled up to his door. "Please forgive this lapse in hospitality but, as I'm sure you know by now, a large meteorite has come to earth quite nearby." He gestured to the South. "I have waited for you before going to examine it—but I cannot wait any longer." He smiled. "Would you care to accompany me?"

"Of course!" Olgilvy gestured. "Come, join us in the carriage!"

A moment later, the three of them were moving with speed toward the meteorite's reported position.

"Did you see the meteorite as it passed overhead?" Holmes asked.

"Alas, no." He gestured with his hands—a movement that revealed a rather blocky box-like device attached to his belt. "I was asleep when it passed over and did not awaken until after dawn."

"You did not hear the explosion?"

He shrugged. "I fear that I am a very heavy sleeper, Mr. Holmes," He smiled in embarrassment. "Not a very useful trait for an Astronomer, I'm afraid."

"Look!" Professor Olgilvy pointed to a spot about a mile ahead of us. "That must be the point of impact!"

They all peered forward to a point on which a number of carriages and other vehicles were stopped by the side of the road. Holmes could see people beyond the line of vehicles, gazing downward.

"How big a crater would you expect a meteorite of that size to leave?" He asked the two astronomers.

"It would depend…" Olgilvy muttered, leaning forward in an attempt to get a better look. "Upon the size and mass of the heavenly visitor."

"Meteorites weighing tons have been found in the Americas," Pierson put in. "I have been shown an image of a crater in the western portion of the country that is said to be fifteen miles or more in diameter."

At that moment, their carriage came to a halt—blocked by those vehicles that had arrived before.

"Shall we have a look, gentlemen" Holmes asked, opening the door.

"Indeed!" Professor Olgilvy jumped down beside him. "I am more than anxious to see what we have here."

"As am I," Pierson said, joining the other men. Holmes noted that he kept a hand on the large metal device attached to his belt. "Let us see what there is to see."

The three of them turned toward the crowd, pushing their way through until they stood at the very edge of the crater itself.

"Why," Professor Olgilvy muttered a few moments later. "This cannot be right!"

"Why not, Professor?"

"Look how big that meteorite is," the three of us leaned closer, peering over the wall of dirt and sand. A long tear-shaped hole stood in front of us—one that was some twenty-feet deep. In the center of the hole stood what Holmes assumed was the meteorite—a rather large oblate spheroid covered in dust and dirt that lay neatly in the center, filling it nearly to capacity.

"A meteorite that size should have created a much larger crater—four or five times this size at the least,"

Olgilvy turned to his right. "Isn't that right, Pierson?"

"I would have thought so," the younger man nodded. "I don't know how..."

"It must have come in quite slowly," Olgilvy reached out with his walking stick—but was too far from the mass in the center of the pit to touch it. "Or it is very light—which would be unheard of." He looked at the two of us. "We must measure and weigh this as soon as possible!"

"It's far too hot, Professor." Pierson pointed out. "It will be some hours before anyone can get close enough for a proper examination."

"I agree," Olgilvy stared at the meteorite. "I would like to get my instruments as soon as possible. Would you," glancing at Pierson. "Be kind enough to entertain Mr. Holmes until I return?

"It would be my pleasure," Pierson smiled at me. "We can each get a nap and a good meal, refreshing ourselves against the work to come."

"I will drive to your home," Olgilvy started back toward his carriage. "And endeavor to return before the sun sets!"

True to his word, the professor had his driver deliver us at the very door to Professor Pierson's home before departing—at a gallop—toward his own abode.

"Come, Mr. Holmes," Pierson beckoned to me. "Let us use the time we have wisely."

Holmes smiled and nodded.

Professor Pierson's home was much like that of Olgilvy, albeit somewhat smaller. Books on many subjects lined the walls of the large den that stood just to the right of the entrance hall. Behind it was a rather small dining room attached to a tiny kitchen. A central staircase led to the second floor that sported four bathrooms and a washroom with, even this far in the countryside, running water!

Pierson led the great detective up the staircase and opened a door near the remarkable washroom.

"Please make yourself at home, Mr. Holmes." Pierson stopped for a moment, almost tittering as he realized the near-joke he had made. "I think we should both get a few hours sleep before returning to the pit. I will instruct my housekeeper to wake us around half-past three so we can have a meal before we leave."

"That sounds quite satisfactory." Holmes smiled and extended a hand around the den. "Although I would love to have time to explore your library."

"Another time, Mr. Holmes. You are always welcome here." He smiled. "Now I wish you a good rest," he nodded down the hall. "I will retreat to my own bedroom for a time."

"Of course," Holmes bowed and entered the room. "Until half-past three."

Pierson smiled and shut the door behind him.

Holmes laid his Gladstone bag on the bed and looked around the room. It was snug but comfortable. After a moment's thought, he took off his coat, placed his bag on the floor at his side, and composed himself on the bed which was, to be truthful, a bit short for one of Holmes stature.

As he relaxed, Holmes became aware of a noise down the hall—the sound of a voice—Pierson's voice.

He wondered if there was someone else there, having seen no one else upon his entrance.

Holmes opened his own door a crack and listened more carefully.

It was Pierson's voice for a certainty—but the other voice was very strange—almost mechanical…

Holmes left the room and moved silently down the hall until he could hear more clearly—but the conversation ended before he reached what had to be Pierson's door and he was forced to retreat to his own room, pulling the door shut behind him before lying down once again on the bed.

There were no more sounds.

Time passed and Holmes became certain that Pierson was asleep. Pulling off his shoes, he made his way silently downstairs and into that book-lined den. He approached a large desk that dominated the room. A moment's work with one of his lockpicks and he had found what he had expected—notes and diagrams of a highly advanced sort.

He stowed them in his voluminous pockets.

Below them was a quite serviceable colt revolver.

He took a moment to render the little gun harmless, then, finding nothing else of interest, returned to his room and, this time, allowed himself to fall asleep.

***

Three-thirty came very quickly. Holmes was roused by Pierson's call. He took a moment to wash his face and hands in that remarkable washroom. Then, refreshed, he put his shoes on, picked up his bag and joined his current host at the dinner table downstairs.

"I hope you slept well, Holmes." Pierson said by way of greeting.

"I did hear some voices at first," Holmes shrugged. "Doubtless you giving your housekeeper her instructions."

"Yes," his brows rose. "That must have been it." He reached for a small bell on the table. "We must hurry our meal—Professor Olgilvy will be here soon and I want to get to the pit before he arrives."

Holmes nodded and unfolded his napkin as a rather dense-looking woman put a plate in front of him.

"It's curried chicken," Pierson informed Holmes as his own plate slid into place. "Her specialty."

"Wonderful," Holmes took a spoonful, chewing carefully. "Quite nice," he told Pierson politely.

In truth, it was a meal that Mrs. Hudson would not have allowed to sully her table—but this woman was in no way equal to Mrs. Hudson.

Holmes endeavored to eat the whole plate, realizing that he might need the energy the meal would provide. A quite normal cup of tea followed and the great detective was soon ready to continue his adventure.

"Are you quite done, Pierson?" Holmes smiled at the man as he sipped at his tea. "You did want to beat Olgilvy to the site…"

"Of course," The Professor took one last sip and stood. "It's a short walk—we shall be there well before the good doctor arrives." He turned toward the door, turned its knob...

"You're taking no instruments?"

"Professor Olgilvy will provide them and, believe me," the Professor grinned and shook his head. "His are far more numerous and ingenious than anything I might be able to provide."

"I don't believe that for a second!" Holmes turned to the door alongside him. "I think you're far more capable of ingenuity than the Professor."

"Thank you, Mr. Holmes." He pushed the door open. "That means quite a lot coming from you.'

A moment later they were in the open strolling down a quiet country lane, undisturbed by either man or beast.

It took only a few minutes to walk to the pit. The crowd of onlookers had thinned, but those that were left were crowded by the edge of the crater, all eyes fixed upon the meteorite within.

"Something must be happening," Holmes pointed out to his companion. "They seem to be intent on the meteorite within."

"Indeed," Pierson nodded. "Let us see what might be happening."

The two of them made their way—rather rudely if truth be told—through the crowd until they were in a position to see into the pit.

It was immediately obvious what was causing all the uproar.

"Surely that's moving!" Holmes said.

Indeed, the upper section of the 'meteor' was turning slowly, revealing the kind of threading that one sees on a jar of preserves.

"What does it mean?"

"It means," Pierson smiled and looked at the detective. "That there are far more things in the universe than you think, Mr. Holmes." He looked at the slowly unscrewing section of the meteor for a moment, then…

"Don't get too close to the pit." He nodded at the crowd around us. "You don't want to get pushed in by accident."

Holmes nodded and started to ask how he knew so much about what was happening.

A loud noise interrupted him and Holmes turned just in time to see the front of the meteor—or whatever it truly was—had come loose and fallen to the ground revealing a dim interior in which, for a brief moment, he thought he saw something move…

Then the crowd moved closer, pushing him aside in their rush to see what was happening.

"What is it?" Holmes asked.

Pierson smiled. "You'll see in a moment."

The crowd moved closer, pushing Holmes and Pierson aside, while chattering to themselves as they stared at the new wonder in the pit.

But that wonder turned to fear as something began to crawl out of the opening.

"What…what is happening?" Holmes stared with the rest of them as a thing—a creature—dropped out of the open end of the meteor and stared up at them.

It was large—perhaps as big as a bear, with rubbery-looking skin of a grayish hue. The face was wide and featured two enormous eyes topping a large mouth.

More incredibly, it had no limbs as we know them, moving instead on *tentacles*—Holmes counted six at least.

It moved very slowly, with great effort, and he could see its chest labour as it fought for breath.

"It's having trouble breathing," Holmes muttered to Pierson who nodded quickly.

"It's the gravity," he told him. "Almost three times that of their home world."

"And where might that be?" Holmes asked—although he already knew the answer.

"Mars, of course." Pierson's smile widened. "These are Martians!"

Before the detective could reply, there was a scream from the pit and he turned to see a 'Martian' tentacle wrapped around the ankle of one of the onlookers. As Holmes watched, he was pulled off his feet and dragged into the pit.

"We have to save him!" Holmes took a step forward.

"No, Mr. Holmes." Pierson's hand tightened on my shoulder. "It is too late—he is as good as dead." He nodded to the pit. "Look!"

Two other creatures had now pushed themselves out of the meteor and were engaged in assembling some sort of device. It was metallic and bright in the last rays of the sun. As Holmes watched, they finished the device and ran a long cable of some kind from the ship to a receptacle on the device.

One of them turned it on.

"My God!" The exclamation was forced out of Holmes. The device was now a bed of rotating blades and, as he watched, the unlucky captive was tossed into their midst.

Blood spurted as he screamed once. More blood followed as he was, quite literally, chopped into pieces.

The crowd backed away but before being forced to move with them, Holmes saw the three 'Martians' turn to a sort of trough on one side of the machine and lean down into it, some kind of proboscis or beak extending from their mouths and into the gruel of blood and flesh.

They began to eat.

Holmes backed away, unable to tear his eyes from the horrible scene in the pit, it was only later that he realized that while his attention was focused on that horror, another, even greater one was about to take place.

"Come, Holmes." Pierson pulled me to one side. "We need to get some distance."

"But, that man…"

"Things will soon get worse." He pulled the detective to a stand of trees perhaps a hundred yards from the pit. "Look!"

Holmes looked back and saw a new device had appeared. This one on was mounted upon a pole of some kind. It was boxy and seemed to be covered with lenses of an odd design.

As Holmes watched, it turned toward the now angry crowd gathering at the top of the pit.

He saw a green glow and heard an odd, high-pitched screech and then…

"AIEEEE!" Men started to scream as a beam of almost solid light came from the new device and played across the crowd. Everything it touched burst into flame!

"That's an optical weapon of some kind," Pierson told me. "It generates a heat ray exceeding 1000 degrees on the Fahrenheit scale.

"How do you know all this?" Holmes turned away as blackened bodies began to fall around the pit. The machine had turned to those running away, catching them in its beam and turning them into ash.

"Come Mr. Holmes." Pierson smiled. "I'm sure you've figured all that out!"

"That device you carry," He pointed at the box on his belt. "It's some sort of communicator."

"Very good." He pulled it out, holding it up. "But it is more than just a communicator—it translates our two languages into a kind of lingua franca that we can both understand."

"You called them here?"

"I did." His smile widened. "I am not happy with the current rulers of this world so I decided it was time for a change."

"You're as mad as your mentor!"

"Ah," Pierson raised an eyebrow. "You know, then?"

"I know that you studied at the feet of Professor Moriarty—and that he was able to transmit many of his notes to you before he and I had our," Holmes thinned his lips. "Encounter on the Reichenbach."

"He thought very well of you, Mr. Holmes. He felt you were a worthy adversary." Pierson shook his head. "I, however, am not so sure—if you knew who I was, why did you come here and put yourself under my hand? I'm sure you could have talked to your oh-so-important-in-the-government brother of yours and had the army on me before my friends arrived."

Holmes pulled out his pipe, indicating what it was before filling it. "Had I done so, what would you have done in return?"

"Why, I would have sent my 'friends' directly to 221 Baker Street and made sure you were unable to meddle."

"And my good landlady and friend might have been injured." Holmes lit the pipe. "I didn't want to risk that happening."

"Then you're a fool!" Pierson's hand slid out of his pocket holding the little Colt. "Before you do something foolish, I checked the weapon before bringing it—and discovered that you had removed the bullets." He shook his head. "Childish." He waved the weapon toward the pit. "Now, if you will just go that way?"

Holmes took a puff of his Turkish blend. "Toward the pit?"

The two of them moved slowly toward the pit indicated until, some feet away, the Professor stopped. "Now, if you'll wait for a second..." Pierson's left hand pulled the communicator out of his belt and touched two buttons.

Holmes watched carefully.

"Friends," Pierson spoke into the grid on the bottom of the instrument. "I bring you a gift." He smiled and looked at Holmes. "Take your time with him—he is quite special."

"So," Holmes said, nodding. "The red button powers the device up and the black one opens communication."

"Very observant," Pierson waved him toward the pit. "Too bad you will never have the chance to test your supposition."

"Oh," Holmes shrugged. "I don't know…" He waited until they were less than ten feet from the pit—and then moved with the smooth speed that always surprised his adversaries. The pipe flicked forward sending hot ashes into Pierson's face. The scientist clawed at them, desperate to keep them from his eyes.

And Holmes stepped back with the communicator.

"Very foolish, Mr. Holmes." Pierson shook his head and raised the pistol. "What have you gained?"

"This," Holmes tapped the device. "The thing I came here to obtain."

"Well, you have it, for whatever good it might do you." Pierson clicked the hammer back. "And now…"

He pulled the trigger.

"I fully expected you to discover that the bullets were missing.", Holmes spoke into the silence that followed. "Once you made that discovery, I knew you would think yourself so clever that you would not feel the need to look further." Holmes reached into his pocket and pulled out a tiny metallic pin. "And so you would not know that I had removed the firing pin."

Pierson growled—and threw himself on Holmes. "You will not escape! My friends are looking for something special!" He clawed at Holmes' eyes. "And they will have it."

Holmes blocked his assault, giving ground, he parried several wild blows and set himself. When the next blow came, he grabbed Pierson's extended arm and thrust his hip into the younger man's hip.

Pierson, off-balance and unready, was thrown toward—and over—the edge of the pit.

"NO!" He screamed as Martian tentacles locked around his arms and legs. "NOT ME!" He struggled as they lifted him from the ground. "HOLMES!" He looked up at the detective. "IT IS HOLMES YOU MUST DESTROY!"

On the rim of the crater Holmes watched as the creatures dragged Pierson to their hideous machine and placed him in the center of its base.

"NOOOOOO! YOU CAN'T!"

A moment later the machine was turned on and Pierson's scream was cut short by the blades.

"Thank you for the gift," an odd metallic voice spoke from Pierson's device. "We will enjoy it."

"Of course," Holmes mumbled. "What can I do for you next?"

"You said you had maps and plans…"

"They are in my home—I will get them and return." Holmes looked at the activity in the pit where odd metallic devices were being unloaded and assembled. "How long until you are fully ready?"

"When your sun rises…"

"I will be here, ready to guide you in any way I can."

"Good." The voice returned. "We will be ready as well."

As he left the area of the pit, Holmes watched as the Martians gathered around their eating-machine and began to slurp at the earthly remains of Dr. Pierson. He shuddered—and turned away, wondering where the nearest postal telegraph was located…

He had a great deal of work to do.

CHAPTER TWO

Dr. Watson had just begun to worry about his friend, Sherlock Holmes, when he received an invitation to lunch at the Diogenes Club. He knew that meant Mycroft Holmes—and he wondered what the elder Holmes wanted to talk to him about.

He hoped it wouldn't be bad news about his friend.

"You have heard of the Martian meteorite?" Mycroft asked as soon as Watson was seated, allying his fears about Holmes.

"Who in London has not?" He shrugged. "I have been following the account in the Daily Telegraph with some interest," Watson sipped from his water glass. "Especially as your brother is somewhere in the area investigating the phenomenon …"

"You have heard from Sherlock?"

"Not in some days," Watson shook his head. "I had hoped that you would have some word…"

"He is safe," Mycroft's eyes met his companion's. "For the moment, at least."

"Where is he?"

"Still in Surrey—at the site of the first meteorite to land."

Watson nodded, then: "Are the newspaper accounts accurate?"

Mycroft's mouth formed a line of displeasure. "Unfortunately, in this case they have been quite correct—in all ways."

"There are Martians?"

Mycroft nodded. "Sherlock was there when they emerged from their cylinder—and observed their terrible weapons in action." Another shake of the head. "So many dead…"

"He has seen their weapons?"

"His report to me tells of a metallic projector that fires a ray of intense heat." Mycroft's lips tightened. "The few surviving witnesses questioned by the government describe it as 'an invisible, inevitable sword of flaming death."

"Surviving witnesses?" Watson cocked his head, waiting for an answer.

"Most of those who made their way to the pit where the thing landed are dead." Mycroft frowned. "The lucky few who were hit by the ray but somehow survived are hideously mutilated."

"Holmes?"

"My brother lives." Mycroft nodded slowly. "Although I gather it was a near thing."

"What will you do?"

"It is already done." He glanced around him. "Her Majesty has dispatched a battalion of artillery to handle the creatures." He shook his head. "Their ray weapon is powerful but, by all accounts, they are physically quite feeble…"

"*NATURE* talked of a difference in gravity …" Watson muttered.

"Whatever," Mycroft shrugged. "One hopes that the military will be able to handle the problem—but it is my duty to consider all possibilities, therefore, Doctor..." He looked into his companion's eyes. "Her Majesty's government has a posting for you."

"Me?" Watson's voice mirrored his surprise as he murmured something about being nothing more than a simple, rapidly aging, doctor…

Mycroft held up a hand to forestall more excuses.

"Doctor Watson, I am quite aware that you are anything other than a *simple* Doctor," a slight smile played across his lips as he uttered the words. "You are a man who has extremely steady nerves and the demonstrated ability to keep his head in a crisis." He raised an eyebrow. "Do not underestimate your gifts, Doctor—my brother never does."

He pursed his lips and took a quick look around. "What I will tell you now is quite secret—you must not repeat it to anyone outside this room."

Watson nodded assent, his eyes locked on the elder Holmes mouth.

"For several years now," he said, glancing around once again. "We in Her Majesty's government have been taking steps to prepare for the next war." He looked at Watson. "A war for the soul of this country, a war with our enemies on the continent."

Watson's eyes widened at the revelation.

"You know as well as I", he continued. "That our 'friends' on the continent have been making their own plans for some time. You worked with my brother as he investigated several of their attempts to steal military secrets." He looked at Watson. "I believe you wrote up one such case? 'The Bruce Partington Plans' was, I believe, the title you used in the Strand Magazine?"

The Doctor nodded. "Surely you don't expect me to emulate such acts? I cannot speak German and my French...."

He waved his hand. "I have *that* sort of agent available to me at any time I wish. I need you for a more sedentary job—one far less active but more suited to your talents."

"What do you have in mind?"

"Those of us who study such things have decided that the next war will be fought with far more dangerous weapons than any we have seen in use thus far." His face soured. "We also believe that those weapons will be used against civilian populations."

"Surely not!" Watson cried. "That would be barbaric!"

Mycroft shook his head sadly. "The Count Von Zeppelin has been working on a machine capable of carrying nearly two hundred pounds of bombs across the channel to England." He sighed. "Perhaps as far as London! And some of his compatriots are experimenting with poisonous gases to be carried by that same machine!" He looked at Watson. "These are facts, like them or not, they are so."

Watson, shocked to his core, said nothing.

"We must be prepared if—when--such weapons are used against us," Once again the big man looked around the room and Watson realized that he was satisfying himself that no one was close enough to hear him.

"To that end," he continued. "We have constructed a series of shelters in London and the near suburbs— shelters that are proof against gas and solidly built, deep enough underground, to be impervious to any possible bomb..."

"Shelters?"

"At the moment there are eight such," he leaned forward, eyes still locked on Watson's. "I..." He shook his head. "Her Majesty would like for you to act as head surgeon in one of them should it become necessary to activate it."

Watson stared at him, too shocked by his many revelations to answer.

"You would be second-in-command of the site. A trained officer from my staff would be in overall charge." He held the Doctor's eyes for a long second. "I would, of course, expect you to aid him in every way possible."

Still trying to make sense of everything he had been told, Watson nodded dully.

"Good," the elder Holmes summoned a wan smile. "It is my most fervent hope that these are merely precautions—that the shelters never see use." He held up a hand. "But hope has no place in this sort of planning."

Watson still didn't trust his own voice—and nodded again.

"It is my solemn duty to see that we are ready for any eventuality." He signaled to a silent waiter who was standing just a short distance away. "And if that means we must create shelters for civilians," he shrugged. "Then shelters we will build." He favored the Doctor with a raised eyebrow. "Before we leave, perhaps a whiskey and soda might be in order."

"Leave?"

"Of course," Mycroft favored Watson with a smile. "You must inspect your new posting as soon as possible. Fortunately, the individual I have chosen as the commander of that facility is free this evening…"

The Doctor sighed and nodded and, just over an hour later, found himself clambering out of a cab in front of St. Paul's Cathedral.

"You've put a shelter under St. Paul's?" He looked around. "I don't see any entrance…"

Mycroft glanced at the cabbie, eyes sharp. "Let us not discuss it out here in the open," he gestured to his right. "Come this way..."

"Surely the entrance is up those stairs?" Watson pointed to the long flight that led to the cathedral's Front door.

"That's not the entrance we need," Mycroft allowed himself a small smile. "To get to that one, you must come <u>this</u> way."

Watson had, of course, visited St. Paul's on several occasions. Most recently for his second wedding.

The Cathedral itself is one of the most famous and recognizable sights in the country. With its dome, it is the tallest building in London and visible for quite a distance.

Now, Watson had only a second to look up at that dome before Mycroft hurried him away from the cathedral and into an alley on the other side of the street.

"It is possible to reach the shelter through the nave of the Church and the catacombs," Mycroft told him as he held a gate open. "But this is the main entrance." He led the way to the far end of an alley where a cellar entrance stood. "Now, if West is on time…"

He knocked on the cellar door using an odd pattern—one knock, then two, then one more. There was a moment of silence before the door silently opened.

"Major West," Mycroft gestured toward the shadowy figure in the opening. "May I present Dr. John Watson."

James Conrad West was a short man who, Watson immediately realized, was wearing boots with cleverly built-up heels. Watson had seen such 'lifts' before—they were designed to make their wearer appear taller to the naked eye.

West might have been unhappy about his height, but the intensity of his personality was more than large enough to fill any room he entered to overflowing.

In point of fact, Watson already knew something of Major West. Holmes had a file which identified him as the Diogenes Club's most active agent--a man who travelled the world on the business of that oddest of London Clubs.

"I have heard of you, Doctor." West offered his hand. "And I have read some of your work in 'The Strand'."

"I must admit that I have also heard of you, Major." Watson smiled and nodded as he shook warmly. "Your work in Tibet…"

"Is still secret," Mycroft interjected as he moved past, gesturing for the two men to follow. "Come. I have little time, there is pressing work waiting for me in Whitehall"

The alleyway entrance opened into a long corridor that ended, a few hundred yards later, at a metal-clad door. Mycroft motioned to West to open it.

"Combination is One-Eight-Zed-Five," he smiled. "Battle of Trafalgar." He pushed the door open. "Remember that."

Watson nodded his understanding and followed, finding himself in a dark corridor that led back in the direction from which they had come.

"The catacombs under St' Paul's are over there," West gestured.

"And under the catacombs…"

"Show him the access points." Mycroft commanded. "I'll wait for you here."

West nodded and, lighting a bull's-eye lantern, guided his now lone companion down a long corridor and through another door that did, indeed, lead to the catacombs under St. Paul's. They then passed between several tombs until, at last, coming to a stone sarcophagus that seemed just a hair cleaner than the others.

"We have to do some more work to do a better job camouflaging this," West said, running a hand over the too-clean surface and shaking his head. "You enter through here..." West pulled the tomb lid open revealing a set of stone steps that disappeared down into the darkness. "Then go down the stairs until you reach another doorway."

"Is there another password?" Watson asked.

"None needed," West raised a hand. "It will be guarded at all times by one of my…" He looked at the Doctor. "One of *our* men."

"I see." Watson peered into the darkness below. "How big is the shelter?"

"Quite large," West gestured to the tombs that surrounded them. "We built a domed ceiling under this level—used some new architectural secrets to strengthen it."

Watson looked at him quizzically.

"The concrete is reinforced with metal bars—increases the strength many-fold. An idea of Professor Challenger. It made construction very difficult but the results are quite good"

"I see."

"The interior of the shelter is designed to hold several hundred civilians. There are rooms for the staff and two substantial dormitories." He smiled and looked at his companion. "As well as an armory and a fully equipped operating theater,"

"Let us hope that we will not need to use that, at least." Watson shook his head.

"Indeed," West nodded. "Let us hope." He opened the door. "Downstairs now."

They entered and went down a long, curving, staircase.

"Here," West said. "Is the shelter."

Watson looked at an enormous dome, made of concrete that was smoothed and finished. The top came very close to touching the ceiling, the interior, he assumed, could be entered through a nearby door.

They paused at the door. "Inside this," West told him. "Is the main portion of the shelter. Over there," he pointed. "Are the command center, meeting room, and…"

At that moment, a young man appeared, his face rather flushed from exertion. "Major? He called out. ""They want Mr. Holmes back at Whitehall. He told me to have you come as well."

"This late?" West glanced at his watch. "Has something happened?"

"There've been new dispatches from Woking," the young man took a deep breath. "The Martians have broken through our lines."

"The artillery…"

"It appears to have been wiped out, sir." He shook his head. "Almost to a man!"

"Damn!" West motioned for me to join him. "Come. We must see what this means."

CHAPTER THREE

As it happened, they did not find out what happened for some little time. It was certain that the artillery had been damaged, even routed. But beyond that, they knew nothing as no new reports came in.

It was eerie. Almost as if the Martians had done something to time itself—but despite this, they waited.

Two whole days passed.

They they found out the grim truth from a British escapee. The Martians had completely broken the British Artillery, killing them almost to the man. Afterwards they continued to come on, unopposed.

Now, two days later, the three men stood on the roof of the naval offices at Whitehall waiting for the walking Death—in the form of the Martian Machines--to arrive.

"There!" West's finger lashed out, pointing at a dot on the horizon. "There they are!"

Mycroft nodded and turned to a naval rank standing at his side, whispering a quick set of instructions that sent the lad running.

He turned back to us.

"I have sent a summons to 'Thunder Child' and 'Warspite' who have been alerted for the last few days," he explained. "If they can catch the Martian machines while they are crossing the river, we might have a chance of stopping them."

"They're much closer now," Watson announced, eyeing the tall shapes on the opposite shore. The three men could see that they were as they had been described in the dispatches from the few survivors of the artillery battalions who had met them two days earlier. Tall, three-legged tripods they were, with a cylindrical cabin on top. They moved with a sort of drunken grace, one leg lifting and swiveling forward while the other two held the thing upright, the movement somehow humanizing them.

"I see three of them." Watson reported.

"They move faster than I would have thought possible on three legs," West had produced a small spy-glass form his jacket and was studying the machines through it. "Although judging by the mechanics of that 'walk', we might be able to trip them using large ditches—much like the tiger traps used in India." He turned to Mycroft. "They would have to be carefully camouflaged, of course..."

He passed the glass to me. "What do you think, Doctor?"

Watson raised the little telescope and looked the machines over. He noted several joints on the legs that might turn out to be a weakness, and the transparent dome at the top..."

"Perhaps the Major is right. Those legs…"

A motion to one side caught his eye and Watson turned the glass toward that side. There, standing alongside one of the oncoming machines was the form of a tall man—a human man. He was speaking into some boxlike device as he pointed forward.

Watson could not make out his face—but there was something familiar about the way he stood…

West reclaimed his glass as the Martian machines grew closer—and more threatening.

"I am not sure they can wade across the Thames!" West remarked. "Their legs appear to be too short."

"We'll soon see," Mycroft pointed to the closest machine which had just reached the edge of the river.

It was at that very moment, other movement caught West's eye.

"Look!" He pointed upriver. "There!"

Following his direction, the other two men saw a ship—an ironclad that lay very low in the water and was moving purposefully toward the Martians.

"That's the 'Thunder Child'," Mycroft noted. "She seems to be alone."

He was right. There was no other warship in sight at the moment although West indicated that he thought he could just make out, in the distance, black smoke that hinted more warships were on the way.

"Can she stop them?" Watson asked. "Does she have the weight of fire?"

"We'll see in a moment," Mycroft pointed at the Martian machines. "Look!"

One of the machines had somehow managed to negotiate its way down the riverbank and was just beginning to wade into the Thames. The three men could now see that several metallic 'tentacles' hung from the base of what they took to be the cabin that held the Martian pilot.

One of those tentacles held the metal and glass box they assumed to be the 'heat ray projector' they had heard so much about, another held a long metallic cylinder, in shape not unlike a cigar.

The 'Thunder Child' steamed directly at the Martians, holding its fire as it came.

The three watching men realized that the Captain wanted to get close enough to make sure he could not miss. The tactic might well have had the added advantage of getting the Martians to hold their fire as, it soon became clear, they did not know what to make of the approaching vessel.

Eventually, the Martian who was already 'knee-deep' in the river lowered the cylinder it was carrying and discharged a stream of black gas at the ironclad.

"That's the gas we've been hearing about," Mycroft said. "It's deadly when breathed in."

The black smoke hit the Thunder Child on her side and glanced off, blowing (thankfully) away from the city. The Ironclad herself drove through the dark vapors and into the clear--almost atop the Martian.

The alien machine backed away, retreating to the edge of the shore from which point it raised the metal and glass box that created the Heat-Ray.

The box lined up on the still-oncoming Thunder Child.

Suddenly, the lenses at the front of the box flared blindingly and a long line of steam sprang from the river, moving toward the 'Thunder Child'.

A moment later the ray struck the ship on its starboard armor, tearing through it as easily as a white-hot iron blade would go through paper.

The 'Thunder Child' was wounded—but not done! An instant later, it fired its guns, point-blank, into the Martian machine.

The Machine staggered and reeled away, one of the legs damaged.

Another volley followed and as they watched, the great Martian machine tottered and fell, sending up a great gout of water and steam.

A cheer went up from those watching from the shore.

The guns of the Thunder Child volleyed again, but the choppiness created by the fall of the first Machine threw off their aim. The shots went wide, tearing holes in the walls of a warehouse to one side of the remaining Martians.

There was no time to reload.

As one, the two waiting Martian machines raised their Heat-Ray projectors and fired. The Thunder Child was caught between their fire and cut nearly in half. Fire appeared on the fore and after deck, and she lost a great deal of her power.

Her boiler was struck by a second volley of rays and, a moment later, it blew up in a great hail of steam and water.

Even at their remove, the three men could hear the screaming of the crew as they fought to get clear. Many men threw themselves into the river, looking for some route to escape.

Some of them were already aflame, their clothing burning as they tried to escape.

To no avail for, just then, a Martian ray tore through the remaining armor and reached the Thunder Child's powder magazine.

The explosion was so brilliant that those of us on the roof were forced to cover our eyes. When we were able to see again, the Thunder Child was gone—only bits of debris and floating bodies marking the place where she had once fought so defiantly.

The surviving Machines ignored the wreckage and made their way across the Thames without further opposition.

There was nothing left to bar them from entering the city.

"There's no stopping them now," Mycroft almost whispered, then turned, his voice stronger. "West! Activate the shelters! The Martians will be using their gas and I want as many inhabitants taken to safety as we can manage!"

The Major nodded and turned. "Come Doctor," he nodded. "It is time for us to take our posts."

Dr. Watson followed, rendered speechless by what he had seen.

***

Away from Whitehall, Watson and West split up—West to open the shelter and start bringing in people, Watson to bring the pre-packaged medical kit from his surgery in Knightsbridge.

The Martians, meanwhile, crossed the river without further opposition. Once ashore, they split up and began to destroy the city. Landmarks were their especial targets and they destroyed them without mercy of any kind.

Parliament, still in session, became a major target. The MP's there barely got out before the arrival of two Martian machines. Many of the men stood and watched as the Martians blasted the houses of Parliament, leaving nothing but burning ruins.

Soldiers, the final bastion of freedom in the city fired on them from positions inside the great clock tower at the edge of Parliament. Their fire meant nothing to the Martians who ignored it while they finished their work, then, in a final gesture, they turned their heat ray onto Big Ben. For long moments, nothing happened, then all at once, the great clock shook, fires sprung up all around and it slowly collapsed on its foundation.

The center of the city was now under Martian control.

CHAPTER FOUR

TEN DAYS LATER:

Watson was tossing and turning as he attempted to get back to sleep, a state difficult to achieve inside the shelter. Despite the best efforts of the craftsman who had built it, the place was damp and chill and constantly echoing with the sounds of the people crowded into the dormitories.

Worse, the never-ending and complete darkness seemed to produce the darkest of dreams—filled with unhappy memories of other, equally dark times--times populated by snakes, and hellhounds, and giant rats that did their best to kill…

Watson's sleep was full of such things so he was nearly ready to give up on any hope of sleep and return to his work when a pounding at the door brought him fully awake.

"Dr. Watson!" A voice cried out. "Wake up! You're needed!"

"I'm awake," He called out, rummaging for a match with which to light the candle he had placed alongside the bed. "Just give me a moment."

"Hurry!" The voice was young and filled with concern. "This is a bad one!"

A bad one. The Doctor sighed as the candle lit the tiny room, illuminating his disturbed bed clothes and the deal table that held too-few belongings brought to this place so long ago.

All of them were 'bad ones' these days, with the Martians marching all over the city.

Watson stepped to the basin of water set on a rough wooden plank laid across two stands—his dressing cabinet and sink—and began to scrub the sleep out of his eyes.

The water in the basin had been sitting for hours and was both tepid and brackish— but it was wet and cold enough to scrub the last vestiges of sleep from the Doctor's tired eyes.

A few moments later, with pants and jacket on and buttoned tight, Watson opened his chamber door to the slight young man he knew would be waiting.

Young 'Bobby' Burns (no relation to the great Scots poet) had been studying medicine when the Martian Invasion began and, when the need for shelters like the one they now occupied became clear, he had clamored for a job in one of them.

Mycroft chose him to assist the surgeon, Dr. Watson, in the main shelter.

He'd done a fine job—but some things were beyond his training and capabilities—which is why he had awakened his superior in the middle of the night.

"Mr. West brought in a number of casualties," he reported, nodding toward the corridor that led to the right. "Two had nothing more than cuts and bruises—we've taken care of them as best we can, but one of them …" He shook his head. "It's horrible!"

"Stay calm, Bob," Watson replied as he motioned him to lead the way. "Tell me of his injuries."

"I don't think I have the words," the youngster answered. "He was hit by a heat ray, but by some miracle, it didn't kill him outright." Burns shook his head. "It would have been merciful had it done so. Instead, it cut through his body, burning away his left arm and half his chest…"

Watson sighed, suddenly understanding the young man's horror. He had seen wounds from heat rays before. They were always bad and this one…

"That sounds like a great deal of damage. You're sure he's still alive?"

"He was screaming and cursing when West brought him into the shelter," Bob shook his head. "He was certainly alive at that point."

"And now?"

"He's breathing—I am sure of that. I can hear his lungs…" The young man hesitated. "I can hear a *wheezing* in his surviving lung as it draws in air one breath at a time." Roberts turned to look into Watson's eyes. "God help me, Doctor, but I found myself contemplating the idea of putting the poor man out of his misery!"

"A natural thought—but something we Doctors cannot do." Watson smiled wryly and gave the boy a fatherly pat on the shoulder. "It is against the Hippocratic oath—and it's well that it is so. Such decisions must lie in the hands of the Creator, not mere men like us."

Watson felt a twinge of conscience as he saw the young man's face relax. He had seen evidence of many doctors 'helping' seriously injured patients escape their agony by easing them into the great beyond. Of course, in this brave new world there were Martian heat rays and the black gas to handle that job for them!

He pushed the thought away—he knew he had no time to think about Martians now—there was a patient waiting. One that, it appeared, badly needed help

"He's over here," Burns led Watson into the chamber that was used for medical treatment. "On the table…"

The chamber was brightly lit by several overhead chandeliers and Watson immediately saw the patient he had been awakened to save.

"Good lord!"

The cry was forced from the good Doctor's throat as he saw what had happened to the man.

"I've given him a little brandy," Burns told Watson. "It seemed to help a little…"

"It's amazing he's still alive!" Watson leaned closer to the table, studying the man's right side—what was left of it.

He had seen many wounds caused by the Martian heat ray over the past few months. They were usually instantly fatal, but this time…

"He must have been gesturing with his arm," The Doctor indicated the movement as he stared at the ruin of the man's upper body. "And was struck a glancing blow from the ray projector…"

The patient's left arm was completely gone as was the lower part of his shoulder. Worse, the umbra of the heat ray had played over the breadth of his chest, slicing away a neat semicircle of flesh and organs--and cauterizing the wound as it went, keeping him alive, but...

The result was quite horrid.

"His left lung's been cut in half," Watson leaned down over the body, biting his lower lip as he tried to understand the extent of the damage. "Part of the rib cage is gone as well as most of the collarbone on this side…"

"His heartbeat is steady and regular," Burns leaned in over the patient, his face pale. "And his right lung is working well enough, although I think it's filling with fluid." He stared at the wounded man's upper body. "But his face…"

"The ray took part of his jaw and most of his cheek," Watson probed at the wound for a moment, backing off as a low moan emanated from the patient. "I don't think it struck his brain or spinal cord."

"What can we do for him?"

Dr. Watson looked over the man's massive wounds and shook his head sadly. "Not much, I'm afraid. He's already in shock—all we can do is keep him warm. When he wakes up, he'll be suffering great pain," Watson looked at Burns. "Prepare a quantity of Morphia in solution. We will need it."

"Yes Doctor." Burns nodded.

"Make sure he drinks all the water he can handle."

"Yes sir."

"We'll attempt to close the wound if he survives the shock although I have never seen one this large." Watson shook his head sadly. "I'll have to work out a way to do it."

"I'm sure you can figure something out, doctor." Burns smiled shyly. "As I'm sure your friend Mr. Holmes would tell you if he…"

"Don't say his name here, Robert." Watson shook his head. "There are those who won't want to hear it."

"Do you think him a traitor, sir?"

The older man shook his head, mouth set in a grim line, thinking about what he had seen alongside the Thames—then pushing the thought away and answering: "Sherlock Holmes was the finest man I ever knew. There is no way…"

"He is most certainly a traitor!" A new voice came from behind Watson. "He betrayed my men to the enemy! I was there! I saw him do it!"

The two healers turned to see a tall man in the tattered remains of a military uniform standing behind them. The bandages on his face and hands told them he was another of the wounded brought into the shelter by the very able Mr. West.

"I am Major Roger Littleford of the Royal Horse Artillery. My battery was tasked with stopping the Martian machines from reaching Whitehall or, God forbid, the Royal Palace beyond." He looked at Watson. "We had reports from surviving gunners who had fought the machines in Surrey. They made it clear that we could not fight in the normal way—in the open, with the enemy before us."

His hand came up, wiped a bead of sweat from his forehead. "It was decided that we would ambush the machines from prepared positions."

He made a gesture. "We set up masked batteries along Whitehall—using buildings and alleys on either side of the street to hide our weapons so that when those damned machines came striding down the street, we would be in the perfect position to blow them off the face of the Earth with massed fire."

He looked into Watson's eyes.

"Then your friend appeared."

"Holmes? You saw Holmes?"

"I did more than see him, sir." Major Littleford shook his head sadly. "I spoke to him and, God help me, listened to what he had to say." His jaw tightened. "I wish that I had ordered him shot as a traitor instead!"

"What did Holmes tell you?"

"He said that we should move out—retreat--immediately. He said that the Martians had machines that would let them see us even when we were hidden behind the corners of buildings and behind trees." The Major glared at Watson, anger building in his face and eyes. "Said they could see our 'heat signature'," he nodded. "Yes, that's what he called it—our *heat signature*." He snorted. "That should have told me what his intelligence was worth."

"What did you do?"

"I told him that we could not move—that we had our orders which, of course, we were honor-bound to obey."

Littleford held Watsons gaze, eyes sparking. "He told me to forget about orders, forget about honor. He told me to pull back now, while I could still save my men."

"I ordered Sergeant Morris," his eyes moved to the wounded man on the table. "I ordered the Sergeant to escort Mr. Holmes away from the area." He glared at the Doctor. "That was my terrible mistake—to allow him to leave!"

The Major's eyes left Watson and turned toward the wall while the memories of the event flooded through his mind.

"Mr. Holmes walked away up the street and, less than an hour later, Martian machines appeared from that same direction. There were four of them and, rather than marching into our trap, they stopped a few score yards short of our position. We could see that their hoods were pointed directly toward us—as if they knew just where we were."

"Holmes would never betray you, there must have been something…"

"I was there, Doctor." The Major whirled to face him, eyes fiery. "I know what I saw!"

He shook his head, memory flooding him. "I watched as the Machines held their position and watched us for a long moment—then the cannisters in their tentacles began to spew out black smoke!"

"The smoke formed into a massive cloud that was like some living thing! It filled the street before us before spilling into the alleys and backyards--racing toward us like…" He gestured hopelessly…

"Like a horde of rats!"

He grimaced. "My men began to cough and choke on the stuff, some falling right where they stood. Others, my bravest, held their breath and attempted to fire their guns…"

His eyes closed. "They never had the opportunity. While we were preoccupied with avoiding the gas, the machines moved closer and were now in position to fire their projectors right into our midst."

He held up a hand. "The gun nearest me exploded—the blast knocked me back against a wall and sent me to the ground. I tried to regain my feet for I knew the gas would kill me if I remained on the ground."

Tears ran down the Major's face as he continued.

"But the gas never reached me. A little eddy of wind ran between the buildings and had enough force to blow the gas away from my gun." He shook his head. "I was lucky…" His eyes met Watson's and he could see the pain of what had happened. "Or so I thought until I saw that the wind was blowing the gas toward the batteries on the other side of the street—and I was forced to watch the men there die in agony when It covered them like a blanket."

Watson wanted to say something—but no words would come.

"It was then that the machines brought their heat rays to bear in earnest. Men screamed as they burned to death." He looked at Watson and Burns for reassurance. "I didn't know what to do. All my training and experience was useless as I lay there, held up by the filthy wall, stunned and sobbing."

"I watched as nearly two thirds of my unit was slaughtered before my eyes." He drew a deep breath. "I watched until I finally recovered wits enough to order a retreat," his eyes again met Watson's. "Allowing some few of my surviving men a chance at life."

"They retreated in an orderly fashion and tried their best to stay out of the sight of the Martian machines but…" He sobbed once. "Many of them died as heat rays swept back and forth over their formation ....”

He bit into his lip. “I would have died with them had it not been for Sergeant Morris there.” He nodded at the wounded man on the table. “The Sergeant threw me over his shoulder and carried me down an alley that led away from the slaughter.” He reached out as if to touch the Sergeant. “That simple action saved my life. A few moments after we left the battery, a heat ray hit the ammunition limber we had laid out ready to use.”

The Major closed his eyes.

“I don’t know how many of my surviving men were killed in the resulting explosion; I do know it did not so much as scratch the nearest of the Martian Machines.”

“What of the other Martians?” Watson asked.

“They were completely unharmed.” Littleford gritted his teeth. “I saw them finish off the remainder of my command before turning and continuing their march down Whitehall, firing their weapons in all directions, burning and destroying the very heart of her Majesty’s government!”

His eyes came back to the Doctor, hard and angry. “I also got another look at your friend, Mr. Holmes, marching at their side.”

The Major looked toward me, eyes full of pain. “I have enjoyed many of your stories in the Strand Magazine, Doctor. I let Mr. Holmes talk to me because I thought he might have some clever stratagem to pull the Martian devils deeper into our trap.” The man stopped, eyes momentarily clouded with pain, and then stared into my eyes.

"I should have shot him, Doctor. For I am certain that he warned his Martian friends about our position—and allowed them to turn it against us …"

Watson stood silent, troubled.

"As it was, only a few of us were able to get away—able to avoid both the Martian rays and the black smoke. We had been given the location of shelters to which we were to retreat if we were in dire need." He looked again at his wounded Sergeant. "It took us nearly two whole days to make the march here. Two days in which I saw things I wish I'd never lived to see…"

"What did you see, sir?" Burns asked.

"I saw turncoats working with the Martians, helping the leathery creatures move when they were forced, for one reason or another, to leave their supporting machines. I watched as men—men like you or I--herded helpless women and children into enclosures circled by metallic fencing—fencing that was faced with sharp pointed barbs like those used in the American west to enclose cattle!" He looked at me, eyes wide and full of horror.

"Once inside the pens, the poor victims were herded to the far side and through a wide door into another, even more horrible metal enclosure. Once that enclosure was full…" He bowed his head, fighting for control. "Once it was full the walls began to close in, crushing the screaming captives, turning them into a sort of bloody paste!"

"Horrible!" Burns muttered.

"Yes, it was horrible. Women and children slaughtered like animals, their blood and flesh and bodily fluids running through runnels in the floor and pooling in what I can only describe as a long trough outside the killing machine."

"A trough surrounded by Martians who dipped their mouths into the bloody liquid." He rubbed his eyes as if to expunge the memory.

"And fed!" Agony filled his face, his voice. "Fed on the very essence of those poor souls. Imbibing their very life's blood!"

"I pulled my pistol out and took aim at one of the creatures…" He sighed and glanced at the operating table. "But the good Sergeant stopped me from firing and held me until I regained my senses." He looked at me. "A shot into that nest of horror would have resulted in both of our deaths, but…" He looked at the wounded man beside them. "I should have taken that shot—killed the damned creature. At least our death would have meant something!"

"How was the Sergeant wounded?" Watson quietly asked.

"We dragged ourselves away from that horrid place and resumed our journey toward the shelter we'd been promised. We had almost reached safety when a single Martian Machine appeared behind us." The Major shook his head. "I froze, paralyzed with fear and horror and would have died right there and then but for Sergeant Morris," another look at the wounded man. "The sergeant kept his head and pushed me to the side—into the shadow of what had been a garden wall. That movement drew the attention of the machine but, before it could move to investigate, the Sergeant drew his pistol and ran directly toward the hellish thing, firing and cursing as he moved." The Major paused, eyes haunted.

"It fired its heat ray at nearly point-blank range—with the horrid result you see." He nodded at his wounded comrade. "It would have been better had it killed him outright!"

"We'll do our best to save him." Watson said.

"You'll do your *best.*" The Major shook his head. "We've all done our best--and what do we have to show for it? My men are dead, my guns are smashed, and my friend..." He bowed his head. "All for nothing..."

"Are you're sure it was Sherlock Holmes you saw?" Watson knew that he had to know for certain.

"I've seen the illustrations in The Strand Magazine." The officer nodded grimly. "It was Mr. Holmes right enough."

Dr. Watson tried to formulate an answer. Anything that might explain his friend's behavior. But there was nothing. Nothing at all he could say.

And that realization hurt him deeply.

He was saved further embarrassment by his patient, who chose that moment to wake—and begin screaming in pain.

Watson hurried to his side, happy to get away from the Artillery Officer.

And quite unable to forget what he had been told.

CHAPTER FIVE

"How could Mr. Holmes have come under Martian influence, sir?" Burns asked as Dr. Watson prepared his notes on the new patients. "I seem to recall you writing that he wasn't even aware that the Earth circled the sun much less knowing about the existence of other planets in various orbits..."

Watson smiled and nodded somewhat sadly. "You're quite right about that," he told the young man. "Holmes believed that –and I quote—'a man's brain originally is like a little empty attic, and you have to stock it with furniture as you choose. A fool takes in all the lumber of every sort that he comes across, so that the knowledge which might be useful to him gets crowded out, or at best is jumbled up with a lot of other things, so that he has difficulty in laying his hands upon it when he needs it.'"

He looked into Burn's eyes. "But while Holmes might not have thought it important to keep facts about the other planets in his memory, the news of the great explosions on Mars was more than enough to draw his attention. He went to investigate them and when the first meteors burned overhead; he accompanied Professor Olgilvy to the site of the first landing.

"Mr. Holmes went to Horsell Common?"

"Indeed. And what he saw there fascinated him. He wired asking me to join him but I was quite busy in my surgery and could not make it." Watson shook his head. "Had I made the journey; I have no doubt that there would now be no question of Holmes' loyalty."

"Was he there when the Martians emerged from their cylinders?"

"He was," Watson thought of the reports Mycroft had received. Reports that described the horrible Martian creatures emerging from their hollow 'meteors' and using their terrible ray machine to incinerate the deputation of local officials who attempted to make peaceful contact with them.

Holmes had been there and Watson had only Mycroft's word that he hadn't been killed with the others, certainly the numbers might have included Holmes—but no...

"Perhaps the Major is right," Burns shrugged. "Perhaps he did throw his lot in with the Martian creatures." He looked at me. "Perhaps it was the only way he could survive."

Watson slowly shook his head, saying nothing.

"You cannot deny that it *is* a possibility!" Burns said softly. "And as I recall, Mr. Holmes himself said that when you eliminate the impossible, whatever remains must be the truth.

Watson signed and turned away, not trusting himself to make an answer—for Burns was right.

And he knew it.

The unfortunate Sergeant died a few hours later. There was nothing that could have been done to save him, his burn wounds were simply too large and too deeply destructive to be survivable.

Nonetheless, the failure weighed upon Watson and so, when the good doctor finished filling out the requisite paperwork (it was, after all, a government installation), he made the decision that it would do his heavy heart and weighty conscience good to take a few moments alone outside the damned shelter to think about all that had transpired.

Watson knew it was dark outside and so told Burns that he would be leaving the shelter for a short time. The young man tried to argue him out of going and, had Mr. West been available, might well have succeeded. But as that worthy was away on a mission, Watson was the man in charge and could do what he pleased.

He reassured Burns that he would stay close to the shelter entrance—within easy call if some emergency arose.

Burns nodded grudgingly as his mentor put a pipe and a quantity of tobacco into a jacket pocket and turned toward the labyrinthine passages that tied the shelter to the catacombs under St.

Paul's.

Her Majesty's Government had not been idle when the Martian Machines emerged from their nest in Surrey and began their march toward London. Early reports indicated that, shockingly, the tripods were more than a match for anything the British Army was able to bring to bear. Soon afterwards, the first reports of the 'black smoke'—the Martian gas that killed anyone who breathed in even a tiny quantity were received.

At that point the Prime Minister ordered that all the prepared emergency contingencies—like the shelter Watson was attached to--be activated while he sent his battalion of artillery out to fight the Martians.

Mr. Mycroft Holmes had some time ago, undertaken the creation of a series of shelters spread around London for use in the European war which he felt was inevitably approaching. Now, he enlisted the aid of both Dr. Lister and the erratic, but brilliant, Professor Challenger to create a counter to the Martian gas.

The two scientists, working as a team, came up with a filtration system that was, they believed, proof against the black smoke and, with the full force of the government behind him, Mycroft had the systems fabricated and installed in a very short period of time, giving the bunkers one more layer of protection to add to their underground locations and hidden entrances.

Sir Christopher Wren's masterpiece, St. Paul's Cathedral, was the home of the first shelter—the one to which Dr. Watson had been assigned. The great architect had designed and constructed a very extensive network of tunnels and catacombs under the nave, the deepest and most remote of these had been quickly and efficiently transformed into something the great man would not have recognized—a huge, concrete dome reinforced (at Professor Challenger's insistence) by rods of iron to form a structure that would, theoretically, stand up to any sort of impact from above now filled the empty space, ready for occupation.

And that was the real problem. The shelter was proof against any danger from *above* but, once occupied, any real problems were going to come, naturally enough, from *inside*.

The air was safe—but it smelled bad and would grow worse as time passed.

The lighting was feeble which, all by itself, caused a sense of unease and, coupled with the all-inclusive damp, would lead to various illnesses that were impossible to treat effectively inside the shelter.

People just couldn't live inside such a construct for very long.

Unfortunately, they couldn't survive *outside* for more than a few minutes.

Watson realized that he'd have to find another way and had been thinking of possibilities since he'd arrived—with no success.

Now, lost in thought, he passed the last in a carefully hidden series of doorways designed to keep the shelter undetectable and emerged onto the moon-lit surface. His gaze fell on the broken pile of stone that had once been the proud dome of the most famous Cathedral in Great Britain.

He had watched it fall from this very spot when a Martian beam, fired from afar and without aim, hit the dome and smashed a hole in the masonry cladding. The air inside the dome heated to such a degree that it expanded explosively, smashing the dome as it did so.

Watson pushed the memory of what had happened to the people inside aside and filled his pipe.

It was quite a pleasant night, cool but not yet so chilly as to require a coat. The air was crystal clear—looking far more like the skies over Afghanistan than those of London.

What most Londoners had come to regard as the normal low clouds and fog were gone and it took the good Doctor a moment to realize that it was because there was no smoke in the air— most of those who lived in the great city were gone—evacuated by the crown or killed by the Martian invaders. The few hardy souls who remained had no wish to reveal their presence by a display of light or smoke— those things, they knew, would bring either Martian machines—or their human thralls—to carry them to a horrid fate.

It struck Watson what a sobering thought that was for a human being, and he took a long moment to consider it. The beauty of the skies above was directly related to the fall of civilization! It was a new concept and one that he studied as he smoked his pipe.

Afterwards, Watson came to believe that he had lost himself in contemplation of the celestial beauty--only thus was he able to explain his almost criminal loss of awareness. One that would have destroyed him had it not been for a happy coincidence.

An unusual sound—that of steam and gears—suddenly brought him out of his reverie. It was a sound he had heard several times before—one that heralded the close approach of a Martian machine.

Suddenly alert, he knocked the dottle out of his pipe, concerned that even that slight increase in heat might allow the Martians to see him—a foolish conceit as he knew that the human body was, at all times, far warmer than the stones and earth around it. More than enough to register on their instruments and reveal his presence.

Watson might as well have held a torch while standing in the illumination of a music hall's lime-lights.

He stood and thought about making a break to the nearby shelter's entrance before coming to the realization that he could do nothing of the kind. Were the Martians to realize that such places existed, they would hunt until they found them, then tear them down and destroy them. The poor souls below would be dragged out like so many pests and thrown into the Martian food processing machines. Grist for the mills.

There was no way Dr. Watson would allow that to happen so, like the soldier he had been, he squared his shoulders, drew himself up straight, and waited for the appearance of the terrible machine he could now hear just beyond the pile of rubble that had once been St. Paul's.

He saw the thing a moment later. A Martian Machine, fully armed and equipped, appeared in front of him--a monstrous thing it was, standing taller than many of the still-intact buildings around it.

The Martian machines were walking engines of glittering metal, and this one was all of those things. It strode down the street, clanking and clanging as the articulate, writhing ropes of steel that dangled like tentacles beneath its hood reached in Watson's direction, the heat ray coming up to hold him in its thrall.

It lifted a foot, heeling to one side. Then that foot came crashing down, smashing one of the statues that had once graced the entrance to the cathedral.

And the thing was nearer. Much nearer.

Watson had seen the machines before—but always from a distance. To have one in front of him, growing closer by the second, filled him with dread and a creeping panic. He had to find a way to escape.

But there was no way out.

One of the tentacles reached in his direction, holding something round. A light suddenly appeared—a cone of brightness that moved across darkness until, after a moment of searching, fell upon the Doctor…

And stopped, holding him pinned in brightness that he couldn't escape.

Watson knew he should do something to at least attempt a chance of survival. Run, flee to one side or the other, do anything that might free him of the blinding light.

But, even with all his wartime experience, he couldn't move. He was paralyzed with an odd combination of fear and wonder.

As Watson stood there staring at the machine he heard a whirring sound far above. He knew it was the heat ray projector rotating to bear upon him and that when it did, it would burn a hole through him as it had to the unfortunate sergeant.

Watson almost—almost—broke and ran for the shelter entrance so close to his side--but he held me still by exerting every iota of will he possessed. He would not allow himself to betray those below—no matter what the cost. Burns and West and the others would not die because Watson had turned coward.

The Doctor stood his ground, holding himself upright and straight, at attention, ready for whatever was to come. His eyes were fixed on the lens of the boxy shape he knew to be the heat ray projector.

A faint light appeared deep inside the thing, dull red.

It brightened…

The hairs on his arms stood up as he faced what he knew to be certain death. Watson fought the fear and straightened his back, gaze fixed on the projector. He was determined to show these damned invaders how an Englishman *should* die!

The light became brighter still and an audible hum came from the device…

Then, quite suddenly, the sound stopped—and the light began to fade away.

Watson sagged, knowing he was to be spared—at least for as long as it would take for the machine to carry him to the nearest 'processing' plant.

He waited for it to move toward him, prepared to fight the tentaclelike metallic ropes that he imagined were already reaching toward him. Watson fell into the fighting posture he had learned in school and clenched his fists …

Then he couldn't help himself. He slumped in relief, almost falling to the ground, as the machine turned and began moving away, walking with that odd drunken stride as it headed deeper into London

Watson knew there must be a reason he was spared but he had no idea what that could be …

There was a movement to his left. Watson turned, squinting in an attempt to see what was in the darkness through eyes dazzled by the light from the machine.

He could just make out a dark-clad figure holding a box-like shape in one hand. The man (for Watson was sure it was a man) walked toward him.

Watson held his ground, prepared for anything, except…

For an instant, the figure was silhouetted against the star-filled sky and Watson could not believe his eyes as recognition flashed through him.

"Holmes?" He muttered, then: "HOLMES!"

He was sure that the silhouette was that of his great friend—he had, after all, seen it many times in the past.

But Holmes, or whoever the man was, ignored Watson's cries and moved quickly away, hurrying to reach the side of that terrible killing machine that had so miraculously spared the Doctor.

Watson stood and watched as the man who, he was certain, was Sherlock Holmes strode down the street at the side of the Martian machine and disappeared into the utter darkness of the night…

CHAPTER SIX-

"You should have come to me before leaving your post!" James Conrad West had been waiting by the door and taken Watson to his office when the Doctor returned. "You have responsibilities, Doctor. You can't just wander off."

"You weren't here to advise me, Major West." Watson told him, avoiding eye contact. "And I needed some time to myself.

"It's a miracle you weren't killed." West glanced down at the report Burns had given him. "I still don't understand how you came face-to-face with one of those damned Martian machines and lived to tell the tale!"

"I must admit," the good Doctor told him. "For a time, I abandoned any hope of being able to tell that story to anyone!"

"Yes," he nodded once. "I can understand that." He turned toward Watson. "At least you had the good sense not to betray the existence of the shelter—or the location of its entrance."

"Sir," Watson stiffened, eyes angry. "I was a serving officer with the 5th Northumberland Fusiliers; I can certainly understand the importance of security!"

"I know your history, Watson." West rubbed the bridge of his nose. "I've read your dossier." He looked up at me. "You served with distinction until you were wounded in the Battle of Maiwand and were sent to hospital where," he paused. "You caught enteric fever while being treated. After that, you were sent back to England on *HMS Orontes* and retired at, I believe, the princely monthly pension of 11 shillings/9 pence."

"I only collected that pension for 9 months," Watson quickly pointed out. "Afterwards, I was able to make my own way through a private practice."

"And your work with Mr. Sherlock Holmes," West looked at me. "Your little escapade on the surface didn't have anything to do with Holmes, did it?"

"Holmes left London before the first cylinder ever fell," Watson told him, unwilling to lie outright. "He never returned to Baker Street."

"Pity." West sighed. "We could use him now." He looked at Watson. "If he hadn't turned on us."

"Did you know Holmes?"

"I met him a few times while working for the Diogenes Club." West looked at Watson, eyes lightening. "A brilliant mind, very nearly the equal of his brother's I believe."

"I would argue the other way on that," The Doctor replied. "I believe that Mycroft's lack of energy makes him slightly the lesser of the two."

"You may have the right of that," West smiled and motioned for his companion to leave the tiny office with him. "But as neither of us can claim to be their mental equals; let us try not to become enmeshed in any foolish adventures." He looked at Watson. "Especially if they involve leaving the shelter and coming in contact with our enemy."

Several things about the shelter had made themselves clear to the Doctor while he was on the surface and now, he realized was the proper time to bring them up.

"I cannot make such a promise," he told the Major. "I have come to the conclusion that it will be necessary to provide at least some small ration of both fresh air and sunlight for our patients and the others who are sheltering here. I believe that if we want them to survive here for any length of time without sickening, we'll have to permit them at least a modicum of both."

"Is that the truth or are you lying to make me accept your mis-adventures?"

"It is not only true, but well documented," Watson nodded. "I can suggest books…"

"No need." The Major waved the thought off. "Give me a report that includes a written estimate on how much time outside the shelter each of our people will require and the two of us can put together some kind of schedule." He shook his head. "It'll be dangerous, but if you say it is necessary…"

"I do indeed!" Watson spread out his hands. "There is no doubt of it--upon my word of honor!"

"Good enough." He nodded. "Get your estimate together and come back with them—until then, you may return to your duties."

Watson returned his nod and left the Major in the corridor, his mind still wrestling with what might have been Sherlock Holmes' actions on the surface and what they might mean to him… And the rest of the human race.

CHAPTER SEVEN

The next few days were uncharacteristically quiet. West's patrols encountered no more survivors and Watson spent most of his free time studying what literature he could find that covered the effects of long confinement without sunshine and their impact on the human psyche.

While he did that, young Burns was tasked with discovering how much time in the sun and fresh air was considered normal for a human being.

Watson delivered the results of their research to West and was immediately rewarded by the Major.

"Thank you, Doctor," he said, glancing at the papers Watson had placed in front of him. "I have decided that you are correct about the people inside this shelter needing occasional exposure to sunlight," he smiled slyly. "Not to mention the opportunity to move around a bit more freely."

"I'm glad you agree," The Doctor leaned forward, a list of those within the shelter in his hand. "Now if you will work with me on a schedule…"

"Later." West waved the papers off. "It is almost time for a little recce through the local portion of the city." He looked at Watson. "I thought you might join us, Doctor." His smile narrowed. "That would allow you to get your dose of sunlight as well as," he glanced at the older man's slightly expanded stomach. "Some needed exercise."

Watson stiffened at the implication (although, down deep he knew it to be true). "Of course," he nodded. "I would be glad of the chance to spend a little time on the surface and walk around, see a bit of the city." He smiled. "Under your supervision, of course."

"Good," West rose from behind his desk. "We leave from the western exit in sixty minutes. Be prepared to spend the bulk of the day outside—longer if we encounter trouble of any kind."

"I will wear sensible clothes," Watson allowed an edge of sarcasm to color his voice. He had, after all, done this kind of thing many times while in her Majesty's service.

"Make sure you have your service revolver with you," West smiled. "Unless you would prefer a more modern weapon?"

"No," Watson shook his head. "My revolver has done well by me all these years and I am happy to continue to depend upon it."

"Good," West waved the Doctor out of the office. "I shall see you in sixty minutes, then."

Watson nodded and left. Burns would have to be briefed and he did want to change into more comfortable shoes…

Fifty-eight minutes later Watson arrived at the door that he knew led to the western entrance. Three other men were already there. He recognized them as Williams, Osgood, and Perry—all members of West's team during his time with the Diogenes Club.

"Dr. Watson," West called out, approaching from the direction of his office. "I am glad you are so punctual."

"I am always on time," Watson snarled, angry at the implied criticism.

"Mr. Burns has been completely prepared to handle the wounded?"

"Of course."

"Good," he motioned to Williams. "Then let us proceed."

It took the better part of twenty minutes to negotiate the labyrinthine corridors and tunnels that led from the shelter to the western exit. The area was huge, and Watson paid close attention to the markings on the walls as they went—he had not used this route until now and he wanted to be sure he could find his way back alone if the need arose.

"All right lads," West stopped the little group as they reached the outside door. "Quiet now…" He turned the wheel set into the door, which, because of the Martian 'smoke' had been built to be as airtight as possible. "Williams first," he ordered. "Then Osgood," he looked at Watson.

"Doctor, you follow them, Perry and I will bring up the rear."

Watson nodded and held his elderly revolver ready as the door was pushed open.

A ray of sunlight shone in, lighting up the rough wooden planking that served as a floor. Watson found me staring at the light, mesmerized by its brightness until…

"Come on, Doctor!" West pushed at the small of the other man's back. "Out you go!"

Watson stumbled forward, catching himself before he could fall and stepped through the door as Williams gestured, alert to any sound or movement in the area round them.

The City of London was spread out before the little group—at least what was left of it. Watson studied the sights, eyes bright as he looked around.

"Blackfriar's Bridge appears to be gone," Watson noted as West came up alongside him. "Was it a Martian target?"

"All of the bridges are gone," he replied. "The Martians want to keep us as penned up as possible."

Watson pondered the implications of that as West formed the little group into a staggered line and led them out on the pre-planned patrol route up Ludgate Hill.

Most of the buildings here were more or less untouched having been too far from the fighting to take any injury. Watson saw that West and the others were watching the windows on either side as they moved down the street and made every attempt to match their watchfulness.

It was more difficult than it appeared. The sun cast odd shadows and occasionally reflected off a bit of metal or a mirror located *inside* a room. That, on several occasions led the Doctor to raise the alarm--much to the amusement of his more experienced fellows.

Watson learned what to look for—and learned how to keep silent if he saw nothing of interest.

They continued the patrol and, before long, reached Fleet Street where the offices of the great London newspapers perched on either side of the road, quiet and deserted while their reporters and editors hid from the Martian Machines and human hunters.

Watson noticed a hint of light and movement in one of the upper windows. He studied it for a moment, but it wasn't repeated. He decided not to report it.

A few minutes later, the little group reached a hill. They made their way up slowly, crawling the last half-dozen feet.

They were lucky they took such care.

"It's a Martian encampment, right enough." West whispered. "They have two, no three of their damned machines on sentry."

"Look at that cage!" Watson pointed, keeping his voice down. "It has dozens of people in it!" He looked at West. "Is there anything we can do for them?"

"No Doctor," he replied. "We are far too few to be of any help." He looked toward the cave. "The men and women trapped there are doomed—and there's nothing we can do to help."

"In fact," West checked with his glasses, then nodded, surveying surveyed the entire property. "This camp isn't finished yet. Look." He pointed. "They're building those globular shelter places so they have a place to relax and sleep." He shook his head. "And, of course, a trough where they can have their food as wanted."

"Amazing." Watson mused. "If these people were not invaders, if they had come in peace, there's so much we could learn from them." He turned to the Major. "They are years ahead of us in all things mechanical."

"That's true," West pushed himself down the hill. "But they are invaders—enemies—and all we can do for now is avoid them." He made a motion to the group as a whole. "Let's get back—we'll check this place again tomorrow."

Watson nodded, then a motion caught his eye. He turned toward it and saw a tall, thin man giving directions to those building the shelters. Watson was sure it was Holmes, but he didn't dare report it. Instead he merely rejoined the other two troops and together they made their way back through the countryside. Watson again thought he saw a motion in the deserted buildings on Fleet Street, but it was over almost before it had begun and he decided it was just a trick of the light.

An hour later, they were back in the shelter.

"What did you think of that, Doctor." West asked as they returned to the control area. "Was it enough for you?"

"Not in the least," Watson smiled. "It was good to see the light—and it would be better to see it again." He looked at West. "Tomorrow at the same time, perhaps?"

"If you insist."

"I do." Watson nodded his head. "I think it is my duty to see the world as it is." He shook his head. "It is certainly different from the way it was."

"Of that, there can be no doubt." West thought for a long moment, then: "You are free to again, Doctor. If you feel it will be helpful."

"I do, Major." Watson nodded again. "I truly do."

"All right," west waved a hand. "Same time tomorrow, same place as well." He looked at Watson. "You may be of some help if we find any survivors."

"Of course." Watson stood. "Then I will return to my duties here—for the moment."

West laughed. "Tomorrow, Doctor. Tomorrow."

Watson walked off, lighter in his step for the time spent in the sun.

It didn't take long before he was found by Burns.

"Doctor," the boy said softly. "It's well you weren't hurt." He stepped a hair closer. "You are needed."

"What's wrong?"

"Some of the older survivors are complaining." Burns explained. "They say they can't take the lack of sun much longer." He looked at the Doctor. "They're threatening a mass exodus."

"They can't do that!" Watson shook his head. "Tell them—no, I'll tell them myself. Take me to them."

Burns nodded and turned away.

Watson followed closely.

***

There was quite a group of survivors waiting. Most were older men, men who couldn't get used to the dankness of the shelter, some of the younger men were having problems with the lack of light. The women had the usual complaints, and added the difficulty of doing laundry and preparing meals in the damp darkness of the shelter.

Not one of them were happy—and they expressed that unhappiness to Watson at great length.

"My grout is killing me!" An older man complained.

"My laundry never gets really dry!" One of the women added. "It's this damned dampness!"

"I can't sleep!" From a middle-aged gentleman.

Watson waited patiently, never saying a word until they were finished, then he spoke quietly and assuredly: "I've given the Major a paper that explains the situation as I," he looked around and saw the anxious eyes. "As we all see it. He forced a smile. "He understands the problem and is ready to put my plan in motion." His eyes swept the handful of people in the room. "It will just take a few days to work out all the problems, but, please," he said with all his heart. "Please wait until we're ready to unveil it. We cannot risk our survival by allowing you to go outside without proper supervision."

They agreed, not altogether willingly, to give the new plan a chance—then filtered back to their spots in the shelter. Watson waited until they were gone, then said to Burns who had stayed at his side. "Keep an eye on those people, Burns. "It wouldn't take much to turn them into an angry mob." He looked at his aide. "And we cannot allow that." He looked around. "It would be deadly in such a small space as this."

"As you say, Doctor." Burns essayed a small smile. "We cannot allow them to riot." He looked at Watson. "I'll keep an eye on them as you say." His smile widened. "It'll be all right I think—they did believe you, maybe that will be enough."

"Perhaps it will." Watson sighed. "And, I believe, it is now time to do our rounds."

"Yes sir," Burns nodded looking at his timepiece. "Whenever you say."

"Let us do them now." Watson took a moment to wash his hands. "While I'm in the mood and they are still waiting for us patiently." He smiled. "As patients should."

They went to the hospital section where he and Burns took rounds as usual, giving equal time to those badly hurt and those there just for the company. It was their usual routine, but took less time now. There were fewer patients then there had been when the shelter was opened, a mark of the care they had received and Watson gave out drugs as needed. Finally, finding himself finished, he retreated to his quarters where, finally finding his bed, he lay down.

And almost immediately, was deeply asleep.

***

The next day, he was up bright and early to join West and his men for their daily patrol. As he had the day before, he scanned the buildings they passed for movement, paying especial attention to one building on fleet street.

He scanned its windows, searching for a change in light, something that would prove he had been right the day before.

Then he saw it—a movement, a real movement. This time, he was sure.

"West," he called out. "Up there, I believe that light moved."

The reflection moved again as the entire team watched.

"You're right," The Major motioned to position his men. "There's definitely somebody up there."

"What is the procedure?" The Doctor kept looking up. "Do we send men in?"

"We have to find out who it is." He moved toward the building. "Martians do not live on the upper floors of buildings—they cannot climb stairs in our gravity." He gave his men a signal and two of them entered the building in question. "So, we seek them out, make sure they're not a threat and take them in if necessary."

"Who might it be, who would be in there?"

The men reached the stairs inside and started to climb.

"It has to be survivors of some kind." The Major kept his eyes on the spot. "We'll soon find out. My men are almost at the proper floor."

Moments later, the men reached the fifth floor. For a moment they disappeared into one of the rooms, then: "There're two of them up here, sir." Williams said, emerging from one of the building's windows. "Brothers, they appear to be."

"Only boys? What happened to their parents?"

"Dead, I believe." He nodded to Perry and Osgood who were escorting two youngsters who, judging by their dress and lack of hygiene, had been living rough for several days.

"Dr. Watson!" West motioned to me. "Can you examine these two and see if they pose any threat?"

"Certainly." Watson moved to within an arm's length of the nearer of the boys, eyeing him carefully. He had, at first, believed him to be a teenager but now, upon closer inspection, realized that while the boy was tall, he was no more than eleven or twelve years of age.

His companion, who was clearly a sibling, was younger still. No more than eight or nine.

"Where, exactly, did they come from?" Watson took a step closer, examining the two in a search for signs of disease or injury—and finding nothing but torn clothes and dirty bodies.

"They were living on the fifth floor," Williams, now down, told him. "High enough to be above the gaze of a patrolling Martian machine while still low enough to reach the street outside quickly if the need arose." He produced a long knife with an odd, downward curving blade that had broken—snapped, in point of fact—at the tip of the blade. ""Here's what caused the reflection you saw." He nodded to the taller of the two children. "The older lad there was holding it when I came through the door."

Watson and West both recognized the knife instantly. They had seen it's like many times in India and other parts of the East…

"It is a Kukri knife, the standard weapon of the Sirmoor Battalion," Watson noted. "The only Indian unit to stay loyal during the mutiny. They are now the 2nd Gurkha Regiment," He nodded as memory flooded him. "The Prince of Wale's Own."

"The knife is mine," the older lad suddenly interjected. "My father gave it to me when he retired from the Army a couple of years ago."

"Your father served in India?"

The boy nodded. "He was with the 92nd Highlanders, sir." His face lit up with pride. "He served under Brigadier Donald Stewart."

"Did he now!" Watson smiled and gave the youngster a pat on the arm. "Good men, the Highlanders." He looked into the boy's troubled eyes. "Where is your father now, son?"

"Dead," the boy shook his head. "My mother, too."

He looked at Watson, eyes haunted—a look far too common in the days since the invaders reached London.

"The Martians?"

"Yes sir." He looked down, fighting the tears that flowed down his face. "My father was trying to get us out of London—we have family in Kent—but when we reached the river, the bridge was down and we knew that my mother and brother would be unable to swim across. We hid from the Martians for a time but when we saw what the black smoke could do," he shook his head. "We realized that we could not stay at ground level—for it was there that the smoke was thickest and most deadly." He looked at West. "My father decided we'd be safer if we could get up high," he indicated the building he had just exited. "This was the tallest building we could find that was open so we took refuge here…"

"Was anyone else in the building?"

"Nobody we saw," the boy shook his head. "My father believed that everyone who lived there had evac…" He bit his lip. "Evac…"

"Evacuated?"

"Yes! Evac-uated before we arrived!"

"So, you were able to escape the smoke."

"Yes sir." He nodded. "We hid on the fifth floor," he pointed. "The smoke finally blew away—which was a good thing as we had no food or water at all."

"What did you do?"

"My father said he was going to forage for what we needed. He told me and my brother here," he nodded at the younger boy. "To stay with Ma while he..." The boy's mouth twitched as he tried to maintain his composure. "While he searched the area."

"Go on."

"He told me to take out the knife," the boy nodded at the Kukri blade.

"And use it, if necessary, to protect my Ma and brother."

"And you did just fine," Watson told him reassuringly. "Just fine."

"No," the boy shook his head. "I didn't do fine at all." He glanced at his brother. "I stayed with Ma and Tommy here as Da had asked. I kept a guard on the door, and a watch out the window." His eyes found mine. "But my Da never came back and we got thirstier and hungrier..." His face folded in upon itself and he looked down at the floor. "We shared what little water we had—it didn't last long and eventually Ma told me it was time for us to leave. She said that we had to find someplace else—someplace where there was water..."

He rubbed at his eyes and looked from West to Watson. "We left here three days ago and headed toward the center of the city. Ma thought there'd be people there—and food."

"That was dangerous," West put in. "The Martians are clustered around the center of the city."

"We..." The boy sobbed now, unable to contain his emotion. "We found that out.

"What did you see?" The Doctor asked, careful to keep his voice soft and gentle.

"We had nearly reached Covent Garden when we came upon a great metal cage," he shook his head. "It was full of men and women," his eyes closed as he remembered. "They seemed to have given up hope and were just lying on the metal floor, half asleep." He looked at me, eyes suddenly burning. "My father was in that cage!"

"That must have been horrible!"

"You don't understand. He was right there and he didn't even see us! We ran forward and Ma yelled his name over and over." The boy bit his lower lip. "That was when the machine came..."

"A Martian sentry?"

The boy nodded. "It had these kind of tentacle things hanging down from beneath it—only they weren't really tentacles, they were shiny--like metal, controlled by the Martian in the cab. Before we could do anything, before we could move, it had caught my mother and lifted her off the ground."

He closed his eyes, fighting the tears again.

"I raced to her side and tried to cut her free..." He gestured to the knife. "But the blade broke and she was gone before I could think of what to do."

"Why didn't it grab you as well?" West asked. "Was there some problem? A damaged Machine, perhaps?"

"I don't know." The boy shook his head. "I was so frightened. I grabbed Tommy's hand and pulled him away, running just as fast as I could…"

Tears streamed down his face now.

"I left my Ma and my Dad behind. I left them in the Martian's hands…"

"There was nothing you could have done."

"Dad asked me to protect Ma. He asked me to keep her safe." The boy suddenly collapsed onto the floor, crying.

"Can you help him?" The younger boy asked. "He's been like that since…" His own eyes brimmed with tears. "Since we saw …"

"We'll help him." Watson put a reassuring hand on the boy's arm. "I promise that we will find a way to help you both."

"There was something he didn't tell you. Something I don't think he saw."

"What's that, son?" West asked.

"When the machine grabbed our Ma, it was about to grab us too but it stopped." He looked at us. "It stopped because of something the tall man did."

"The tall man?"

The boy nodded. "There was a tall, thin man standing beyond the cage. I saw him when the machine grabbed Ma."

"What did he look like?" Dr. Watson was suddenly sure he knew the answer to that question.

"Tall, thin, a kind of long nose…" The boy looked at the Doctor. "He had this funny metal box in his hand—small with a thin bar sticking up in the air." The boy nodded as he remembered. "He talked into that box and the machine backed away—left Edward and me alone."

Watson was sure he was describing Sherlock Holmes but didn't give any sign to West.

"You've both had a difficult time of it," He said, instead, then turned to the Major. "We should take them back to the shelter, I think I have all that I need to handle their needs stored away there."

"You handle it, Doctor." West directed. "Williams will guide you back while Osgood and I continue the patrol."

"Be careful," Watson told him in earnest. "It sounds as if the Martians have created a new nest somewhere in the vicinity of Covent Garden."

"I believe you're right, just as I believe we saw the place last night." He smiled. "But I need to be sure, which is why I need to have another, longer, look." He motioned toward the two youngsters. "Take care of them and I will see you upon my return."

"All right."

"Be careful, Doctor." The Major laid a hand on the Doctor's shoulder. "I wouldn't want you to end up in a Martian cage."

"Nor, I assure you, would I!" The very thought of that event brought a tingle to the good Doctor's spine that didn't subside until they were safely back in the shelter.

CHAPTER EIGHT

"That young man was talking about your friend, Mr. Holmes, wasn't he?" West asked Dr. Watson after he had returned from his scouting sortie some hours later.

"What makes you say that?" The Doctor temporized.

"Come now," he looked at Watson with shrewd eyes. "We have received a number of such reports. All talk of a *thin man with a box*," his eyes bored into those of Watson. "A man who is always in the company of the Martian machines."

"That proves nothing."

"Dr. Watson, you're blinding yourself to the facts." West leaned closer, eyes hard. "Your friend Holmes has given his soul to the Martians, everything we have found points to that."

"Is that what you think?" Watson shook my head. "To me it appears that he *stopped* the machines from grabbing the two youngsters and adding them to the group in that horrible cage, how is that proof of collaboration?"

"That could well be true," his expression remained unchanged. "But if it is, why didn't he save the boys' parents as well?"

"Perhaps he could not."

"Or would not," West shook his head sadly. "I hope your analysis is correct, Doctor. I really do. But I can't help but think otherwise."

"Sherlock Holmes would never work for an enemy of humanity," Watson told him. "Never."

West shrugged and stood, then hesitated for a long second before turning back to the Doctor.

"If I see Mr. Holmes giving aid to the Martians, I will have no choice other than to treat him as an enemy—and, like any other enemy, kill him where he stands."

With that, West turned to the door—but he had not reached it before horrid screams of terror erupted from the dormitory. Watson abandoned what was left of his meal and headed toward the screams as quickly as he could, West a step or two in front of him.

Reaching the men's dormitory, they found Martin, one of the two youngsters that the group had brought back, barricaded behind his overturned bedstead, eyes terrified as they stared at something only he could see--something so horrible that he cried out at the very sight of it.

"Get him back on the bed!" Watson told Burns as they met in the doorway. "I'll prepare a sedative!"

"Don't hurt him!" Tommy, the younger brother cried out to the men. "It's just a dream. He's had them before!"

"Don't worry, we won't hurt him." Burns motioned toward two other young men— members of West's just-returned crew—to join him in circling the screaming youngster. "We'll just..." Together the men suddenly rushed forward, prepared to pick him up and set him back upon the bed.

Burns was able to get close enough to get a grip on the young man's shoulder while Osgood reached out to grab the boy's free arm. But before he could touch it, the boy moved with lightning speed, the glint of steel visible as he swung at the scout.

Osgood cried out in pain, recoiling as blood spurted from the back of his hand.

"Careful!" Burns called out. **"He's got that damned knife!"**

The warning came none too soon. Perry, the second of West's men, leaped backwards as the knife flashed in his direction, leaving Burns to face the blade's razor-sharp edge alone.

He had no choice but to release the boy and take a long step back.

"What can we do?" Burns asked me. "We can't leave him armed while he's in this state!"

"Get an unused mattress!" Watson answered quickly. "We'll use it to pin him against the wall long enough that we can get the knife away from him! The rest…"

"No," Tommy called out. "Let me!" He stood up, took a step toward the wild-eyed figure of his brother. "He won't hurt me!"

Watson was none too sure that was true but he nodded permission even as West motioned Burns to get the mattress.

"Come on, Martin!" The younger brother intoned as he took a step toward his brother. "It's me—Tommy. You wouldn't hurt your own brother, now would you?"

"Tommy?" Martin's eyes drifted toward his brother's form—as did the broken point of the Kukri knife. "Is that really you, Tommy?"

"Who else would it be?" The youngster took another step forward. "You said that we had to stick together, didn't you?"

"Those things, Tommy! They got Ma…"

"I know." The boy took another long step forward. "I was standing right alongside you when it happened." Another step. "I know it wasn't your fault. There was nothing you could do to stop them…"

"Da told me to guard you and Ma." He hefted the knife in his hand. "He gave me his knife to do it with…"

"It's okay, Martin. We're among friends now…"

"I should have done something. Should have found a way to save her." He looked at his brother. "I should have done something!"

"There was nothing you could have done." Tommy was less than a step from his brother now. "Just put the knife down and Dr. Watson here," he nodded in the Doctor's general direction. "Will help you." He produced a wan smile. "He has promised that he will help both of us."

"I'm not sure …"

"Come on, Marty." Tommy was an arm's length away now. "Put the knife down and let's get some sleep. Tomorrow we can talk about going back to save Ma and Dad."

"Tomorrow." Martin nodded once. "Yes, we'll talk about it tomorrow." He lowered the knife. "I'm so tired, Tommy. So very tired…"

A moment later, he slumped against his brother's chest, unconscious or asleep.

CHAPTER NINE

"I'm glad no one got badly hurt," West said as Burns and Watson met with him an hour or so later. "I'm told Williams got nothing more than a minor cut…"

"I've already seen to it," Watson assured him. "He'll be fine with a little rest." He looked at the Major. "Give him a couple of days off."

"And the boy?"

"I gave him a fairly strong sedative. He should sleep for several hours." Watson leaned forward. "It's what happens when he wakes that worries me."

"What do you mean? What's wrong with him?"

"Young Martin isn't the only one in this shelter who has been forced to watch a loved one fall into Martian hands." Watson spread his hands in an inclusive gesture. "Nearly every individual we've taken in is dealing with the trauma of that experience. They are coping in whatever way they can," He looked at West. "For the moment."

"It's your job to help them stay fit in whatever way you can, Doctor." He replied. "Physically and mentally, you understand that?"

"I <u>am</u> doing everything that I know how to do now." Was the answer. "But it may not be enough." Watson sighed. "We must find a way to give them hope for the future—elevate their morale."

"How do you propose we do that?"

"This *cage* the boys speak of," Watson looked into West's face. "Did you find such a place on your patrol after I left? Was it the one we saw in the Martian encampment the previous night?"

"I believe it was," West nodded. "But I was careful not to let us get too close." He made a gesture. "There were several Martian machines patrolling the area—too many for us to be able to get close enough for a thorough examination."

"So the Martians are guarding the cage?"

"It certainly seems so." West frowned. "Why do you ask?"

"It seems to me that the cage and the area around it have no *military* purpose." Watson raised an eyebrow. "It is merely a place for the Martians to rest and build up their stocks of food…"

"Humans—including the boys' parents and who knows how many other poor captives will be crushed to death—made into a kind of porridge for the Martians to devour!" He looked at West. "It is a singularly horrible way to die."

"We cannot save them, Doctor. You know that I was given very strict orders from Mr. Holmes," he gave me a sidelong look. "Mr. *Mycroft* Holmes to avoid doing anything that might cause the Martians to notice us." He shook his head. "I'm sure beginning a military operation of the kind you suggest would go against those orders."

"Mr. West, your little patrols are enough to bring the Martian notice on us." Watson smiled. "And it may be that we are now the only organized group in this city *capable* of any sort of military operation!" Dr. Watson leaned forward, eyes hard and sure. "If that is, in fact, the case, surely it is our *duty* to harry the enemy whenever and however we may." Watson waved a hand. "Not to mention rescuing whatever civilians we may in the process."

"We have no artillery, no explosives…"

"Neither of which, as you and I are both well aware, are of any use against the Martian machines." Watson tried a sort of smile and waved a hand. "I know we cannot do any good with an outright assault—but there may be other ways."

"Doctor Watson, if you can think of a way in which we can damage the Martians without killing the people I'm sworn to protect, I definitely want to hear it." He leaned back in his chair, tenting his fingertips.

"Pray elucidate."

"You know that such things are not my area of expertise."

"Nor mine, Doctor." West shook his head and sighed. "At least not exactly. I will, however, give it some thought and I hope you will do the same." He looked up and gave me a quick smile. "For now, though." He stifled a yawn. "Good night to you."

CHAPTER TEN

Watson spent a great deal of his time over the next few days talking with the two youngsters. Martin was still having difficulty sleeping and, although the others in the dormitory were sympathetic, it was clear that they were not happy at having their sleep constantly interrupted by the young man's nightmarish screams.

The Doctor talked to him every day, trying to convince him that there had been nothing he could do to prevent the capture of his parents--but it seemed to do no good. His conscious mind had come to accept that he was not guilty but some other part of him—a part Watson believed he might call the 'Sub-Conscious' was not willing to forget.

A few days later, Watson discovered just how badly he had failed.

West had agreed to allow the inhabitants of the shelter a few hours in the sun (or what passed for the sun in London) once or twice a week. It seemed to raise morale and the poor souls under his care began to smile once again.

Then, one day, when it was the turn of Martin and young Tommy to go outside, the smiles disappeared.

"Dr. Watson!" Burns rushed into the good doctor's 'surgery', interrupting him as he removed William's bandages. "The boys! Martin and Tommy!" He slammed into the edge of Watson's table; eyes wide. "They're gone! They've run off!"

"Damn!" Watson quickly rolled up the last of the dressings on William's hand, made sure that the wound made by the Kukri dagger had fully healed, then: "Williams! Go to Mr. West. Inform him that we have a problem!"

"Yes sir!" He nodded and quickly left the room.

"Now," Watson turned to Burns. "Tell me exactly what occurred, how did they manage to break free?"

"It is unimportant how they got away," a familiar voice replied from behind. "What is important is that you find those boys before they reach the Martians."

Watson whirled to see the familiar form of Sherlock Holmes standing in the doorway of his surgery.

"If you fail to stop them," he said. "They will bring the Machines down upon you." He shook his head. "And there will be nothing I can do to help."

"Sherlock Holmes!" West had just arrived. His hand pulled out a sidearm, holding it securely, but not pointing, it toward the detective. "What are you doing here?"

"It is time," the detective said. "To tell you the entire story." He looked at West. "You have been in touch with my brother, I believe?"

"I have. He has told me quite a bit—including the fact that you might be a little more than you appear to be. But I will tell you, that business with the Captain and his artillery…"

"My brother is understating things a bit—and that Captain was a fool." Holmes brought himself to full size. "You know I have been working with the Martians?"

West twitched slightly, the gun shifting restlessly. Then he bit his lip and kept the gun where it was—at his side. "I have heard some things…"

"Contact Mycroft," Holmes smiled. "Tell him 'Sherlock has come in from the cold," he turned a bit toward the Major. "And requires some help to finish his mission." He looked sternly at West. "Don't waste time--make that contact at once!" He smiled chillingly. "I promise to still be here when you return."

West nodded tensely, took one more look at Holmes, then holstered his gun, turned and headed to the communications center.

"Now Watson," Holmes said. "It is time you knew the whole truth!" He took off his hat and settled back…

By the time West returned, Holmes had revealed the story of the past few weeks to Watson—including his entire strategy for the future …

"…And when we studied the information I returned with and discovered that…" He shook his head. "It led nowhere, but…" He turned to West who had just re-entered the room. "Are you satisfied, Major?"

"I am, Mr. Holmes." He nodded. "Quite satisfied, although why you cut all communication with humanity…"

"Elementary," Holmes locked his gaze on West. "If I did not communicate with people, there would be no communications that might reveal me to the Martians." He shrugged. "Quite simple really."

"And now?" West asked.

"Now I have a problem." He looked at West then turned his gaze on Watson. "Two problems in fact."

West sighed and said. "According to your brother…" He looked at Holmes. "Your problems are mine to help solve." His eyes narrowed. "What, then, exactly, are these problems, sir."

"First," Holmes said. "You have—or rather *had*--a boy here who is planning to betray you to the Martians."

"You mean young Martin." West nodded. "He has been giving us a difficult time but doesn't appear..."

"You are wrong." He reached into his pocket, withdrew a pipe. "He is in their power." He filled the pipe. "You have to stop him before he can return to them—or he will turn in everything he has learned in order to…" He shrugged and lit up. "Protect his parents."

"I see," West sighed and began to make a note. "And the second problem?"

"I need a Martian—alive and ready to test my new discoveries upon." He smiled. "It's the only way to be sure…" He turned on West, eyes bright. "The only way!"

CHAPTER ELEVEN

"You see," Holmes told them over a hot cup of tea a few minutes later. "Mycroft and I have been trying to find a weakness, either in the Martian machines or their life support systems." He took a sip. "Unfortunately, nothing has appeared despite all our searching, however," he took a sip. "I took the time to check on the living conditions of the Martians—their home environment and all that might mean here on earth." He looked around. "Their atmosphere is dry, their landscape seer and lifeless." He shook his head. "It caused me to begin to think about their true selves." He smiled. "So, I began thinking about *biological* weapons." He looked at them. "And believe I have discovered some that might work. So…"

"And so," Watson put in. "You need a live Martian to test it on."

"Indeed," Holmes nodded. "I have decided that we cannot defeat the Martian machines, they are too powerful, but…" He took another sip. "We may be able to beat the Martians themselves."

"I believe I see what you are driving at," West noted. "But capturing one of those things will be very difficult." He sipped his own tea. "Damn near impossible as far as I can see."

Holmes smiled. "I agree it is difficult, therefore…" He finished his cup and looked up. "When do we start? Those boys are out first problem."

West smiled wryly. “I agree.” The smile widened. “Would tonight be too soon?”

And so, it was that two hours later a small band of men made their way out of the wreckage of St. Paul’s and silently headed for the Martian encampment, searching for one small boy...

“Keep the noise down,” West said from the front of the group. “We don’t want to expose ourselves.”

“I have done what I can to keep the Martians out of this area,” Holmes said. “They believe my claim that it is irradiated.”

“Irradiated?”

“Apparently, such things are quite common on Mars.” He smiled. “My little machine gave me quite a little information about radiation and its effects on vital organs.” He shook his head. “Nasty stuff. I’m glad we haven’t moved that far.” He looked at West. “As yet.”

West snorted. “They must be insane to bring such things upon themselves,” he shook his head--and continued onward followed closely by Holmes, then Watson, Williams, and Cutler bringing up the rear.

“Almost there,” West motioned with his hand. “It is odd that we haven’t seen any sign of the boys as yet.”

“They are here,” Holmes stated. “A little ahead of us.” He motioned to the ground. “Their tracks quite plainly give them away.”

West nodded and they continued on. Through the group of damaged houses they went, sidling up to the very edge of the cleared space. There West knelt low, his weapon ready. “The nest is just ahead." He looked at Holmes. "Right over that little rise."

"Yes," Holmes dropped down next to him. "That would be the place." He looked around. "Now how can I get a Martian to come to me back at the shelter…"

"Let us take a look." West began to crawl forward. "The rest of you, stay back…"

Holmes followed and, a moment later, the two of them reached the crest of the little hill.

The Martian camp stretched out before them.

"Our two boys have arrived before us," Holmes pointed to the quiet forms of Martin and his brother approaching the Martian fence.

"We must stop them!" West thundered, lifting his pistol. "They know far too much."

"There may be a way…" Holmes suddenly stood. "Wait here and, for God's sake," he strode toward the Martian Encampment, "Do not fire a shot!" He began pulling out the little machine he carried in his pocket.

Watson had climbed the hill by now and, together, the men watched as Holmes moved closer to the Martian camp, walking openly and muttering something into his device. The guard machine took notice and turned in his direction, raising the heat ray…

Holmes ignored it. He continued to talk and, finally, strode beneath the guard machine which, like an obedient dog, returned to its initial position.

"That was close," West muttered. "I wonder what he told the Martians."

"I don't know," Watson shook his head. "Some kind of intelligence. Maybe, places to attack or something of that kind…"

"Look!" Williams pointed to his right front. "It's the children! They're moving!"

Sure enough, the two kids were marching dutifully toward the Martian camp—and they had gained the notice of the guard machine which was tracking them as they came forward.

"What do we do?" Williams said. "They're close!"

"There's nothing we can do now," West spoke, eyes hard. "All we can do is return to the shelter and move the survivors elsewhere. Then we,' he shook his head. "Hope for the best." He looked at Watson, his face drawn. "I should have ordered those children locked in from the start…"

"Wait!" Watson cried out. "There's something happening…"

Inside the Martian encampment, there was movement. Two of the big machines had come to life and were moving toward the front gate where the guard machine was blocking the boy's path.

"They're stopping the kids from entering," Williams said. "I wonder if they'll use the heat ray…"

"Look at the kids!" West noted. "They're backing up."

"They look surprised," Watson said. "As if whatever they were going to tell the Martians has become worthless."

"It's Holmes," West pointed. "He's telling the Martians something about those children!"

"Let's hope they listen!" Watson breathed.

"Whether they do or not," he motioned to his men. "We'll have to grab those two as soon as possible."

"Indeed," Watson nodded. "They must not have a chance to get through to the Martians."

"Williams! You and Cutler," West motioned. "Get down there—stay out of sight."

"Right."

"And what do we do?"

"Stay right here," West nodded toward the camp. "And see what happens…"

For a time, nothing much did. The two children, rejected by the Martian guard, stood despondently in place for a time but finally backed away and withdrew…

A moment later, they were captured by Williams and Cutler who pulled them clear of the Martian camp. West motioned for his two men to take the two boys back to the shelter and they soon disappeared back beyond the deserted houses.

Meantime, every Martian Machine in sight had acquired a rider. They had all turned on their lights and were looking around the camp. Watson and West wondered what they were looking for, and finally gave up wondering and waited for Holmes to return.

It was some time before he came back up the hill--he was accompanied for a large portion of the trip by two of the huge alien machines. They went with him as far as the main gates at which point, he said something into his device and they turned away.

Moments later, he had reached out position.

"Holmes!" West hissed. "What in blazes just happened?"

"Walk behind me," Holmes said, not turning our way. "Keep out of sight."

With nothing else to do, we followed Holmes away from the Martian camp and into the darkness of the deserted buildings where he stopped.

"That's better!" He finally said, turning to face us. "I was afraid one of them would see you—that would have spoiled everything."

"We got the boys," West told him. "Although I'm not sure what happened to them back there after they left us." He shrugged. "if all went well, they're on their way back to the shelter."

"I told the Martians that the boys were making an attempt to free their parents. Naturally, they were turned away…" He pulled out his pipe. "Especially as the Martians executed their parents some days ago."

"They're dead?"

Holmes nodded. "Like a good many others." He looked at us. "If we don't find a way to stop them soon, that will be a preview for all of us."

"But, Holmes…"

"No, my friend. The shelter will not fool them for long. Even now they're working on a machine—a 'ground-piercing radar'—that will be more than enough to find us. No, if we do not defeat them soon, they will find us and…" Holmes paused. "Eat us, each and every one."

We continued on our way, silent now as we took in what he had said.

CHAPTER TWELVE

We re-entered the shelter some thirty minutes later. Holmes had insisted that we vary our path to make it impossible for the monsters to track us. So, we zig-zagged through the deserted buildings, went up one street and down another until we once again found out way to the wreckage that had been St. Paul's.

We then made our entry on the South side, passed through the casket strewn area directly beneath what was left of the church and found ourselves in the shelter.

"The boys," Holmes asked. "Do your men still have them?"

West turned away, "I'll find out." He left the chamber.

"Damn it, Holmes." Watson said. "What are we going to do with those boys? And a Martian!"

"Do, Watson?" Holmes relit his pipe, puffing at it until it was burning at an even rate. "We are going to make sure the children are safe and locked in, then we must capture a Martian after which, with a little luck, find out how to defeat them." He took a puff. "Failing that…"

"We will all be killed," West said re-entering the room. "The children are here, held in one of the rooms we designed for that purpose."

"Good," Holmes took another puff. "I am ready to get a little rest." He looked at West. "Can I depend upon you to wake me early tomorrow…or rather, this morning?"

"Of course." West nodded. "Come, I'll show you a place where you might lie down."

"Thank you," Holmes looked around. "But this will do." He laid himself on the settee. "Get me up in four hours—we have plans to make and no time to waste!"

With that, he put his pipe out and laid down, asleep before his head hit the pillow.

"Why don't you join him, Watson." West asked me. "We could all use the rest."

"And you?"

"I still have some reports to do." He looked at me. "Do not worry, I will be all right, Doctor."

"I doubt it, but…" Watson shook his head. "I'm too tired to argue about it." He stood and walked out toward his room. "I will try to get a little sleep, at least." He turned back. "As should you, West."

"I will, Doctor." He yawned. "I need it too."

CHAPTER THIRTEEN

The next morning, Watson checked the condition of the boys. They were healthy enough, but their memories--and the truth of the Martian intrusion ran deep…

"I have to go, Doctor!" Martin said. "My parents…"

"Are dead." Holmes had entered the room. "Killed and eaten by the Martians."

"No!" Martin looked at him. "I won't believe it."

"Believe it," West followed Holmes. "Mr. Holmes saw it with his own eyes."

"It is true," Holmes said. "And I am not likely to ever be able to lose the image of that situation…"

Martin stared at him.

"Your father died like a man." Holmes stated it simply. "He stood there as the machine ground him up." Holmes eyes were haunted. "He did not cry out, even as the blades cut deep. Your mother…"

"No…" Martin stared at him. "No!"

The youngster burst into tears.

"Come, Holmes," West stepped forward, took the great detective by the hand. "Let us plan for the defeat of those devils." He started to lead him out. "Dr. Watson will care for these young men."

They left the room together.

CHAPTER FOURTEEN

As it happened, it was almost an hour before Watson was able to join them once again.

The Doctor had done his best for the two boys, talking with Martin and trying to get him to let go, forget about his parents. Finally, he had been forced to leave them, lightly sedated, in the locked and guarded room.

"It'll be best if we speak with them again as soon as possible." He told Holmes and West in the main room. "We have to convince them of the truth of Holmes story—that the Martians killed their parents and…" He looked at Holmes. "Ate them."

"It shouldn't be hard," the detective said, striking a match. "It is, after all, the truth." He lit his pipe. "And not what we have to worry about at present." He pulled out a pen. "We have to have a Martian—and this might be the way." He laid the pen down on a piece of paper. "This, is what remains of St. Paul's Cathedral." He drew a square in the center of the paper. "The Martians know we are in this general vicinity but not exactly where." He puffed on his pipe. "That lack of information is the one thing that keeps us alive." He puffed again. "I propose bringing a war machine right up to our door," another puff. "And taking the Martian from it, alive and conscious but unable to hurt us."

"How would we do that without getting ourselves fried by his heat ray machine, Holmes? Will you ask him nicely?"

"That is precisely what I plan." He drew his box out of a pocket. "This device allows me to talk to the devils, as long as they think I am working for them, we have a chance."

"They didn't see you last night?"

"They saw me," Holmes puffed some more. "But they did not really see the boys—or you." He drew some lines on the paper. "I think I can get them to come if I ask."

"And how do we get the Martian out of the machine?" Watson asked as he arrived.

"That," Holmes gave him a little smile. "Will not be a problem. I will simply go inside and push him free" He looked at the two men. "Now, if you will help."

"I am with you, Holmes." Watson said. "Always."

"I am not in your thrall like Doctor Watson," West smiled a bit. "But I too will put my future in your hands, Mr. Holmes--I have decided that it does need to be done."

"Good." Holmes sat back. "Then we'll try it today, around twilight." He pulled his little box out. "Now let us see if the Martians will comply…"

CHAPTER FIFTEEN

The Martians would, it seemed, be ready to comply with almost anything Holmes proposed.

His message, sent through that magical little box, got a quick and positive reply. A Martian machine would, it promised, make an appearance at the time and place he proposed.

West and his men began the preparations, and, within an hour, had the site prepared for what was to come.

At the time designated, Holmes stayed in the open, certain that he would be protected by his box. He found a convenient spot and lit his pipe, settling on the ground and waiting.

For the rest of the crew, it was not so easy. West had arranged for two dug outs to be created, each facing the trap we had set. These holes were only big enough for two, so Williams, Cutler, and Watson had to compete for the second hole.

Watson, with his comparative experience—and medical knowledge--won one of the seats. The other, after some argument, went to Williams, leaving Cutler to withdraw into the shelter.

"All right, men." West finally said. "We don't know when this machine will come or what direction it will come from." He looked around. "Get seated and make yourself comfortable. It might be a long wait."

The four men picked their spots, then settled in. West was right, they didn't know from which direction the Machine would come—and they had to be ready for anything.

Time passed. An hour. Two…

Then there was a clanking sound…

"That's him! Coming from the East." West snorted. "Everyone get into you assigned place!"

The men all settled deeper in their hidey holes. All save Holmes who stayed where he was, pipe aflame, puffing away, seemingly unworried about anything that might happen.

"There it is!" Williams whispered. "On the right, near the main street."

The Martian Machine was indeed there, striding along as if it had not a care in the world. And perhaps it did not—as yet.

Watson looked at the trap. Would the Alien machine fit? Would it even come up this high on the hill? If not, their trap would have been for nothing…

He waited and watched.

The Machine stopped…

Like a flash, Holmes came to life. Showing a gusto the men in the dugouts had not seen, he rushed down the hill to the Martian's side. He was expostulating into the little box all the way, although it seemed to do little good until he was within a dozen yards of the Machine…

Which again started to move.

Holmes flashed us a sign behind his back—it was okay, the Machine was going to crest the hill.

Watson settled back to wait, sure his friend had everything under control.

And, for the moment, Holmes did. The machine strode boldly up the hill, looking steadily forward until it was only a little way from the trap…

Then it stopped. The huge head swept back and forth for a long second…

Then, satisfied, the machine strode forward. One stride, two, then it's left front foot hit the trap. It struggled for balance for a long moment…

Then fell with a crash.

The entire group rushed forward, yanking at every potential opening they could see.

"It's this one!" Holmes snapped at us, pulling a hidden door open, and showing us the dank inside where a multi-armed Martian tried desperately to turn the heat ray in our direction.

"I'm afraid not!" Holmes said, rapping the Alien hard with a long metal pole he had hidden to one side.

The Martian fell, squealing.

"All right," Holmes turned his gaze toward Watson and the others. "Let's get it out and properly caged."

"What can we use that will hold it?" Watson asked.

"I think I have something," West nodded. "Mr. Holmes brother told us it might be necessary."

"Get it—quickly" Holmes was inside the Machine now, squatting alongside his prisoner. "I'll push him out…"

It took a little time but, eventually, West unloaded and assembled a lightweight cage that was just big enough for a recumbent Martian.

Each of the men took a part of the aforementioned alien and, not long after, the Martian was our prisoner.

"Keep an eye on him," Holmes warned. "While I get rid of the Machine."

"You know how to operate it?"

"In theory," Holmes smiled. "I've seen enough of their operation to have some idea how it works."

West nodded. "Good luck."

Holmes just waved and, a few moments later, clanked away—unsteadily—in the Martian machine. He was gone for well over an hour and when he returned, he told the group that he had left the machine next to the British Museum—if this trial succeeded, it would make a fine exhibit.

By then the Martian was stirring, and Holmes went to his cage, interested in what he was thinking.

"I can use this little box to talk with him," Holmes told Watson and West. "It translates English into its Martian equivalent and, when he replies, it does the opposite."

"So, you can, with minor problems, speak the language?" West said, brows knitted.

"Essentially," Holmes looked at him. "You are correct." He lifted the box. "Let us see if it works as it should in this situation."

He took out his little box and, while West watched, spoke into it.

"Martian," he said. "Tell us, are you frightened?"

The translated noises, heard following his words, meant nothing to us.

The Martian, however, had pushed himself up and was staring at Holmes, his huge eyes unblinking.

The little box translated his reply: "Should I be, pale one? What do you plan for me?"

“I’m going to test out a number of things on you,” Holmes answered. “Dangerous things.”

“Can you keep me hidden from my people that long?” It returned. “They will look for me.”

“Not for a while.” Holmes answered. “Perhaps they will give us enough time.” He shut down his box. “Come,” he said to West. “Let us get him under cover.”

Without another word, the three men each grabbed a part of the loaded cage and carried it into our lair.

CHAPTER SIXTEEN

West, Watson, and Holmes retired to the command room once they had gotten the Martian under cover. It was time to see if they really had a solution to the Martian problem.

Holmes used the small radio to contact his brother, telling him (in a few short sentences) that he had captured a Martian and that it was time for the others to come to the shelter.

West asked him who the 'others' were—but Holmes ignored him, lighting his pipe and retreating to the back corner of the room where he sank into one of his black thought processes.

He was still there, puffing away, when the others left to try and get some sleep.

Morning found him still there, still puffing.

"Damn it, Holmes!" Watson spat out. "You can't just treat us like dummies—we should know who these 'others' you've called in are."

"Watson," Holmes looked at him. "You of all these people know my methods. Who do you think we need to finish this experiment in a positive way—with the Martian dead?"

"Why," Watson got a pensive look. "You've told us the Martians are invulnerable in their machines. That must mean that you have some sort of idea about using…"

At that moment, the outside sensors picked up movement. Holmes stood and tapped out the dottle that remained in his pipe.

"Unless I am very wrong," he said. "Those will be the 'others' you are so concerned about."

"Who are they, Holmes." Watson stared at the doorway. "What do they know that we do not?"

"They know far less than we do," Holmes laughed. "But they know more than enough to come when called."

That was all he would say. A moment later, he was gone, heading for the closest entrance to those movements. West went with him while Watson was forced to stay behind and do his rounds.

"Who do you think they are, Doctor?" He was asked by Burns as they completed their rounds. "Any idea?"

"I suppose we will find out straightaway." Watson answered. "After all, they cannot keep their identity secret once they get inside, can they."

"I would think not." Burns said, nodding thoughtfully. "I guess we will know soon enough."

"Indeed," Watson grinned. "Come, Let us go and find out who they are."

Burns smiled and, matching Watson's move, started marching down the passage that led to the command center right behind his mentor.

They would find out who the 'others' were, one way or another.

CHAPTER SEVENTEEN

"So, Watson," Holmes greeted them. "Say hello to my brother—and your benefactor--Mycroft."

"Mycroft Holmes!" Watson took the offered hand. "It's been far too long!"

"Indeed," the older man said. "West leads me to understand that you've done well here. Perhaps we can find you a more important job. Now that Sherlock has come in, he might have a suggestion or two."

"I am fine here," Watson answered. "Although I'd like to see more of your brother, I understand his importance to our survival…"

"It may not be important for much longer." He turned to the two figures alongside him. "Allow me to introduce Dr. Lister…"

Lister bowed and extended a hand.

"And Professor Challenger." He looked at me. "Brought from his retreat for just this purpose."

"Gentlemen," Watson said, bowing. "It is an honor to meet you—indeed, an honor to meet both of you!"

"They—and I--will be testing various things on our Martian." Sherlock explained. "Various diseases and so forth." He looked at me. "Perhaps you'd care to help?"

"Of course," Watson answered. "Anything I can do…"

"Good," Holmes smiled. "Tomorrow morning then, around eight."

Watson nodded.

"Till then, doctor." Lister said. "Good night."

"As you say, doctor." Watson smiled. "Have a quiet night."

The next morning, Watson made his rounds as usual, then, giving his other duties to Burns, he hurried down a hallway to the place the Martian was kept. He was met by Sherlock Holmes and Dr. Lister.

"Watson," Lister greeted him. "I'm glad to see you looking so ready!"

"Indeed, Watson," Holmes added. "It's as if you expect to win the Martian War singlehanded!"

"It is not that," Watson said, a bit embarrassed. "It's having a chance—maybe finding a way to actually kill them…"

"We understand, old boy." Holmes smiled. "We do understand."

"Now," Professor Challenger said, coming through one of the doors. "Let us get to work."

Work this day consisted in enlarging the Martian cage and making it transparent.

Watson labored away with Homes, West, Challenger, and Lister. He used some wooden bracing to hold the transparency in place, adding strong metal locks at any place that might open inadvertently.

Slowly the new cage grew.

"I have to take evening rounds," Watson said after several hours had passed. "Have no fear, I shall return shortly."

“Go ahead,” Lister smiled at him. “With a little more work, we might have it finished by the time you get back.”

“Due, of course,” Holmes added. “To your excellent work to this point.”

Watson beamed, and nightly rounds went very well indeed until...

“It’s Martin, sir.” Burns had been aiding him when he could, and was now facing him. “He won’t eat—won’t do anything.”

“And his brother?”

“He’s fine. It’s just Martin.” Burns shook his head. “I don’t know what’s going on in his head.”

“Let us see.” Watson decided, turning to the room the two youngsters were locked into. “Unlock it, if you please.”

Burns quickly complied and Watson stepped in to find the neat room turned into a near-disaster area. Clothes had been thrown about willy nilly and the various items placed there to maintain cleanliness—toothbrush, comb, and the like—were everywhere.

The boy Martin was sitting cross-legged on the bed, his face black. Tommy sat at his feet, full of regret and something else--perhaps a touch of bitterness.

“What’s the problem.” Watson asked as he strolled in. “Martin, what have you done to your room?”

No answer.

“Tommy,” Watson turned to the younger boy. “What is it, has…”

“ARRRGH!” Came from Martin as the young boy came to life and leaped upon Watson who, surprised, went over backwards, which allowed Martin to leap over him.

"Stop him!" Burns yelled as Martin regained his feet and sped down the hall. "Don't let him get away!"

He turned to Watson. "Doctor, are you all right, Doctor…"

Watson nodded, struggling to get his feet under him. "I'm fine—catch the boy!"

By now the entire center of the complex was involved, some moving here, some there, all of them confused and surprised.

But Martin had disappeared.

"Where is he, Tommy?" Watson asked. "He can't have gone far."

"I don't know, Dr. Watson. He won't talk to me anymore."

"We have to find him," West had just arrived. "He cannot be allowed to give our position to the Martians—especially not now!"

"Martians," Sherlock Holmes was a step behind West. "What about the one we have here?"

"Of course!" West turned. "Williams, Collier…"

Two men appeared.

"Go to the cage, make sure our prisoner is secure."

"And if they find the boy?" Holmes asked.

"Take him in hand." West told his men. "Don't hurt him if you can help it."

"Let us follow them, Watson," Holmes said as the men raced off. "We have to be sure our capture is secure."

"Holmes…"

"Now, Watson." Holmes stepped away, moving swiftly down the hallway. "We must go now."

Watson nodded and followed, mind a little muddled.

"Come on, Watson." Holmes told him. "Hurry along." He smiled. "It's not that far."

Watson nodded again, and sped up to match the speed of Holmes.

"He's heading for the captive Martian," Holmes called to Watson. "If he gets there first, he will cause great trouble for our project."

"How, Holmes?"

"The Martian is helpless now, but if he finds even the most rudimentary machinery…" He shrugged. "The mind boggles at what he might do."

"Ahead and to the right," West, just behind us, shouted out.

"Let me go first," Holmes said. "I believe I can control the Martian if he is free of the cage."

"If I can get a shot…"

"No." Holmes uttered the phrase blankly. "He must not be killed."

"But if we can't keep him secured…"

"Just hold your fire," we were almost there now. "I will handle it, never fear!"

We turned the final corner just as Martin, face red with exertion, finished opening the last of the locks on the Martian's cage.

"Damn!" Holmes said entering the area. "I had hoped…" He advanced slowly, eyes on the barely moving form of our captive.

"Holmes!" West said, coming to a halt. "We can't let it get away!"

"And we will not," he stepped forward. "We just have to…" He suddenly leaped at the cage, hands reaching for the cage fasteners. "Lock it before he can move!"

Watson and the others moved in, each reaching for one of the fasteners which clanged shut, holding the Martian fast.

"There," Holmes said. "That will hold our captive." He turned. "And as for the boy…"

Martin stood there, not more than a foot away. He was poised on the balls of his feet, ready to run or fight…

"Stand easy, Martin." Holmes said quietly. "There's nothing else you can do."

The boy looked hard at Holmes, then, suddenly, he started to cry.

"That's all right," Holmes took a step toward him, a hand outstretched. "I understand."

The boy looked up into the detective's face. "How can you?"

"Because I too have felt the Martian Invasion in a special way." He produced his little box. "For a time, I helped the Martians—but that time is over."

"Over?"

"We have the weapons we need; it is only a matter of time until we defeat the invaders."

"And my parents?"

"We shall avenge them." Holmes promised. "You have my word."

Martin, eyes full of tears, looked at Holmes. "I…I believe you."

He fell into a fit of crying.

"Take him, Doctor." Holmes said to Watson. "He won't cause you any trouble."

With that, he turned away and headed for the Martian. "Time," he said. "Is short."

CHAPTER EIGHTEEN

While Watson escorted young Martin back to his room, the dignitaries that had appeared yesterday joined Holmes.

"Are we ready?" Lister asked.

"We seem to have everything we need," Mycroft said. "Aside from the samples you and the good Professor have brought."

"What shall we try first?" Lister said. "I feel sure that the smallpox will be effective, but there is a case to be made about cholera as well."

"Neither will go first," Sherlock said. "I believe we should try one of the oldest of Earth's diseases." He smiled. "Let us try the common cold, it would be easiest to explain."

While the others watched, he took a vial of liquid and dropped it into a culvert that entered the room.

"That's good," he said, watching as the liquid moved inside. "Now we must wait…"

"Only until tomorrow," Mycroft said. "Then we will try the Smallpox sample."

The others seemed satisfied with that and as one, turned and headed back to the main base.

***

The common cold apparently did nothing to our Martian friend, so the smallpox was administered and the men withdrew again.

That didn't work, so they put in the cholera—then it was yellow fever—then polio. Nothing seemed to work until, upon the morning of the twelfth day…

"Okay," Holmes said. "It's time to try some combinations—the cold and smallpox didn't work individually, but we'll mix them together and see what happens. He made the proper moves at his lab table and took the finished serum to his Martian friend. "Try this…"

The serum went into the cage.

"We must wait some more," Holmes said. "I'm sure this is the proper way to destroy them, it is just…"

"You must relax, Holmes." West told him. "You haven't slept in days, your mind…"

"I'll sleep when we're done," Holmes replied. "For now, I have work to do." He continued to putter with the jars full of deadly disease germs. "One of these has got to affect him."

It took time. The team used germ after germ, the Martian grew thinner, robbed of its usual food. Finally, in the dim hours of morning, Holmes tried one more dish…

The effect was remarkable!

"Look at that!" Watson was the first to see the Martian's response. "He's going crazy!"

Indeed, the captured Martian was experiencing throes of some odd kind, its skin palpitating noticeably.

"What did you give it, Holmes?" Dr. Lister asked.

"Normal cold germ mixed with anthrax." Holmes smiled coldly. "Which seems to work."

"Indeed!" Mycroft entered the room. "Look! It's dying."

The Martian was indeed dying. As the men watched, its throes slowed down, the palpitations running across its skin became more pronounced—then slowed down until, after a few minutes, they were still.

The Martian was dead.

"It works!" Mycroft breathed. "It really works!" He turned to his brother. "Can we make enough of this stuff?"

"We can." Holmes stated, smiling. "And we will."

"We'll be ready in a week," Dr. Lister added. "No more."

"Good." Mycroft nodded. "Then we'll schedule pickups for eight days hence." He nodded again. "And may the Martians mark the day!"

'September eleventh." Holmes looked at the body. "Will be the last day on Earth for these monsters."

"Let's get to work!"

CHAPTER NINETEEN

Holmes and his two companions worked feverishly, combining large amounts of germs in the lab then rendering them into bundles that were held inside compressed air tanks. It took days to get it right, days in which Holmes and his little group did not sleep and seldom ate.

Finally, on the sixth day, there came a break in the activity.

"That's the last one," Lister said, holding a tank in his hands. "The last one…"

"London will be safe at last," Holmes said. "And we'll pass the information to the rest of the world…"

"No, we will not." Mycroft said. "We cannot let the thing we have done here pass to anyone. The world must never know.

"But the Martians in France. In America…"

"We will send troops with the proper armament," Mycroft said. "But the rest… It must stay secret."

"Why?" Watson asked. "It's just a bunch of germs…"

"Indeed," Mycroft answered. "Germs packaged for delivery—which would work anywhere for anyone." He looked at the Doctor. "Think of our friends the Germans acquiring this. Do you think they would hold off using it? No. We would be fighting the use of this forever!"

"I see…" Watson nodded. "It's too dangerous to let them know."

"Indeed," Mycroft replied. "We dare not let word get out. If this works, it will be done by God."

"The simplest things he placed upon this Earth." Watson nodded. "Yes, I see."

"Good. Now," Mycroft made a motion. "Let us get this completed—we're running out of time. If the Martians should happen to find us now…"

"They won't." Watson nodded. "We already have this done. Once we spread it…"

"It'll be over." Mycroft looked at him. "Once we spread it."

***

Morning seemed to come early on September eleven. Holmes, of course, was already awake as was West. Burns woke Watson at seven o'clock.

"Are we ready?" Watson asked.

"They say they are, Doctor." Burns answered him. "Just waiting for you and Dr. Lister." He smiled. "They aren't bothering Professor Challenger—they said he was more trouble than he was worth."

"He was a bit of a handful," Watson pulled on his heavy trousers and reached for his boots. "Tell

then I'll be ready in a moment."

True to his word, Dr. Watson joined the others in the main room a few minutes later.

"Good Morning, Doctor." Mycroft greeted him. "I trust you got some rest."

"I slept well enough." Watson replied, grabbing the cup of coffee Burns fetched for him. "Are we actually going to do this? Now? Today?"

"Of course," Holmes told him. "Why would you think otherwise?"

"No reason, just…" Watson took a sip of the coffee. "Just prepared if things weren't ready."

"Everything is prepared," Dr. Lister told him. "We have tanks of the stuff for each of us. Now…"

"Now is the moment when we spread it in the Martian lairs." Holmes said. "The quicker, the better."

"Can we get all of them?"

West answered, spreading out a map. "Here are the Martian strongpoints." He pointed to several red dots on the paper. "You can see that most of their forces are within twenty miles of London." He looked at Watson. "We will use that to our advantage."

"The Martians have never seen anything like this," Lister noted. "They will be shocked and, soon after…" He smiled. "Dead."

"And may God help them all!" Mycroft added.

"Are we ready?" Holmes asked.

"As soon as men from the other shelters arrive." West said. "Which should be right about…"

There was a shiver of alarm as one of the outposts registered something.

"That should be the men from Southampton." West rose. "I'll bring them in."

The alarm went off a second time.

"And that should be the boys from Norfolk." West headed toward the exit. "I'll bring them all back here."

"Be careful," Holmes called after him. "The Martians are not dead yet…'

West ignored him and exited the shelter, re-entering some few moments later leading six men.

"These men are from two of our shelters," he told the room as he came in. "We have not yet heard from the other two."

"We probably won't," Mycroft stated. "We had to accept a high percentage of casualties when we set these up. Nobody answering from the other shelters would lead me to believe they were breached..."

"Leaving us to save mankind." Sherlock stated. "I think we should start as soon as possible."

West agreed, as did Lister, and the group of us went forth to the work shelter.

"Grab a tank," Holmes told the others. "Strap it on."

The men from the other shelters did as they were told, strapping on six of the large tanks."

"Now,"" Holmes went up to one of them. "We have nothing to test this against since out subject," he nodded toward the dead Martian. "Can no longer participate."

"When did he die?"

"Yesterday," Mycroft Holmes answered. "In the early part of the day."

"Less than 24 hours ago." The man nodded. "Good."

"Do you know how to use this?" Sherlock asked.

"I believe so." The man took up the exhaust device. "I aim this in the proper direction, then..."

He pushed the release.

Nothing happened.

"Good try," Holmes had a pistol in his hand. "Too bad it's a dummy."

"You bastard! If I could have killed you…"

"The Martians would have rewarded you handsomely." Holmes nodded. "I know the story. Now back away…"

"The other men from the outside shelters," West looked at them. "Can we trust them?"

"I believe that all but that one," pointing toward the man who had tried to release gas in the building. "Are all right." Holmes took a long look at the others. "Although we'd better give them their tanks outside."

"Yes," West nodded. "I quite agree."

They took a moment to immobilize the traitor, locking him in the same area as Tommy and Martin, then moved outside the shelter.

"Now, gentlemen," Mycroft said. "We'll give you each a tank."

This was done, quickly and efficiently.

"If you'll examine the release…"

Five pairs of eyes studied the device.

"All you have to do is hold it open for a few minutes. Pressure—and the weather—will do the rest."

"Do not release in the rain." Lister added. "Falling water will render this useless.

"Other than that," Sherlock smiled. "I think you have the idea—the Martians, however, will be surprised."

"Any questions, gentlemen?" Mycroft asked.

"Will it harm the populace?" One of the men asked.

"I don't think so," Sherlock answered. "It might give them a cold, but the smallpox is too diffuse to be of harm to anyone," he shrugged. "Beyond that, I cannot say."

"That's good enough for me," the man who had asked the question said. "A far better chance than they might have with these monsters running loose among us."

He reached for one of the tanks.

One by one, all of them studied their devices. One by one they nodded their heads, understanding how the device worked.

"Good." West stated. "Now get back to your shelters and use the gas against the Martians."

As one, the five men turned and headed back into the early morning fog.

"And now," Sherlock Holmes held up a hand. "Let us take care of our own Martians."

An hour later Holmes, Watson, and West each had one of the tanks on his back. They set out toward the Martian encampment.

"Let me go in first," Holmes said. "They still trust me."

"Perhaps," Watson spoke up. "That is no longer true after your treachery the other day."

"They cannot know it was me who called that machine."

"You don't know that." West spoke for the first time. "Better to take them from the outside in."

"It'll take longer."

"So, it will take longer," West shrugged. "It's foolproof—something <u>your</u> plan is not."

"But..."

"No buts, Holmes." West stared at him. "For once, do as you are told."

Holmes looked at West for a moment, then nodded. "All right, we'll do it your way." He moved forward, tank on his back, spout at the ready. "We'll reach the guard posts soon—don't let them see you…"

The men moved stealthily forward, coming to a halt a few hundred feet from the Martian Machine that stood guard on the camp.

"This one is mine," Holmes announced before walking into its sight. He kept on as if the tank were normal and everything was the same as always.

The Machine watched him come, seemingly uninterested, then when he was very close, the hood moved toward him.

Holmes kept on moving until he was on a level with the machine, then he waited for the hood to come closer…

With one movement he slipped his applicator into an opening at the base of the hood and turned on the gas.

The machine stepped backwards, as if human. It tried to lift off its hood, tried to bring its heat ray to bear… Then it froze, the life within gone.

West and Lister followed Holmes into the camp. As one they inundated the globes where the Martians lived, with gas, killing the occupants as they went, until…

"That guard machine is the only one left," Holmes pointed. "I don't think my prior ruse will work as well with him, especially if the pilot saw any of our actions."

"You're right." West noted. "He must know we're killing his people. How do we get to him?"

"I don't know." Holmes said. "Suggestions?"

"We can let him rot on the vine," West said. "Stay in that machine until he needs food."

"He can kill an awful lot of people with his heat ray." Watson added. "We can't give him the opportunity to do so."

"There may be a way," Lister looked at the others on the team. "If we use a human being as bait…"

Holmes nodded. "That might work."

"Indeed." West looked at the others. "But who will be our candidate?"

"I'll go," said Holmes. "I'm the obvious choice."

"No." Watson shook his head. "Too much has fallen on you already. This time, I will go."

"Are you sure?" West looked at the machine. "He may just use his heat ray as you approach."

"IF he does," Watson took his tank off. "You can just let him rot." He placed his gear on the ground. "But for now." He stood up. "Let us see what he will do." He left the cover they had found and moved forward, making no attempt to hide himself.

For a long second, nothing happened. The sentry stood there; the machine cowl pointed at Watson. Then…

"He's powering up," Holmes cried out. "Getting ready to move."

The cowl of the Machine moved as the legs came into play. It took a step toward Watson…

The heat ray turned on its mount.

"Getting ready to fire," West said. "We only have a second…"

"That is all we need," Holmes said. "We just have to wait until…"

The Machine took a step toward Watson. Another.

"Now!" Holmes yelled.

As one, Holmes and West flew into action. Watson fell to the ground, pushed by Holmes. West ran by, his tank of contaminant ready.

The Martian Machine stopped, fired its heat ray just as West got the tip of his applicator in place. There was a long second of chaos, the heat ray going everywhere, then…

"He's dead." Holmes declared. "The last one of them."

"That shot came far too close," Watson said, looking at the smoking scar in the earth. "Far too close."

"We have to remove the body from the Machine." Mycroft stated. "And get the others from their various abodes."

"To make sure we didn't miss anyone." West added. "Then we'll move on the next nearest Martian base."

"It'll take a little time." Mycroft said. "But I believe we'll be rid of these things within a week or two."

"The end of the Martian's time on Earth." Holmes looked around. "Done in a matter of days."

"They took over England in a matter of days," West said. "It is only fair that we reciprocate."

"And we tell everyone that they died, not from our action, no." Holmes stood and looked around.

"We tell them the Martians were killed by the simplest things God put on our green Earth."

"Amen to that." Watson stated.

"Tell the public a big enough lie," Holmes added. "And they will believe it."

"I hope they do." Mycroft looked at the little group of men. "For it will result in a far safer world for all of us."

"For how long will it last?" Holmes stared at his brother. "How long will they accept your fairytale."

"Until the danger is over." Mycroft picked up Watson's tank. "Until the danger is over."

They headed for the next Martian nest…

EPILOGUE

It took some time—years, in fact--but the Martians were done for. Their nests fell to our conquering troops one by one until there was no trace of the Martians left in London, then England.

Troopers, hand-picked and led by West, then did the same job in Europe, freeing first France, then Poland and Russia, and finally, even the Germanies from Martian influence.

None were allowed to remain.

Sherlock Holmes, pleased with the job he had done, returned to Baker Street where he and Watson continued the Adventures they had begun so long ago.

But time was not on his side and Holmes, tired of the same routine, finally left London and began his work with bees. He now lives in Suffolk, happily engaged in bee keeping, a full-time job, it appears.

Major West, promoted to full Colonel for his services against the Martians, led the troops that ended the Martian plague. Upon his return to England, he started and led a special group of British soldiery, one that took on whatever special duties the government found for them.

They came to be called MI-6 and have, for some years, been the governments best hope for the avoidance of new wars.

Watson's young assistant, Burns, went on to a Medical School where, with the help of both Drs. Watson and Lister, he quickly rose in his class until, finally, graduating as the highest-ranking student in history.

The government, ever vigilant, found him a job in the Palace where he has worked ever since.

Mycroft Holmes put upon his friend, Herbert Wells, to write a history of the Martian invasion. He made sure the use of biological weapons was never mentioned.

Wells himself left out the Martian's dietary habits.

He also left out Mr. Holmes involvement, perhaps because he didn't know how deeply he was involved.

The book does state that the Martians were destroyed by 'the littlest things God put on his green Earth.'

Neither did Holmes make a claim upon the concept.

THE END

Doug Murray is married
to Tom's cousin, Pam
Martini Murray. Doug is
the author and Pam
did the cover art.

Christina + Tom
December 2020